A *HORSE* NAMED SKY

A *HORSE* NAMED SKY

ROSANNE PARRY

ILLUSTRATIONS BY
KIRBI FAGAN

Greenwillow Books
An Imprint of HarperCollinsPublishers

A Horse Named Sky
Text copyright © 2023 by Rosanne Parry
Illustrations copyright © 2023 by Kirbi Fagan
Back matter horse photographs from Getty Images—p. 224, Konrad Wothe; p. 227, Mlenny; p. 228, Frank Staub; and p. 229, Bryant Aardema—bryants wildlife images.
Map by Ryan O'Rourke

The text of this book is set in Berling LT Std.
Book design by Sylvie Le Floc'h

Library of Congress Cataloging-in-Publication Data

Names: Parry, Rosanne, author. | Fagan, Kirbi, illustrator.
Title: A horse named Sky / Rosanne Parry ; illustrations by Kirbi Fagan.
Description: First edition. | New York : Greenwillow Books, An Imprint of HarperCollinsPublishers, [2023] | Includes bibliographical references. | Audience: Ages 8-12. | Audience: Grades 4-6. | Summary: Young wild colt Sky must find his way over rough terrain to rejoin his family after being captured for the Pony Express.
Identifiers: LCCN 2023020160 | ISBN 9780062995957 (hardback) | ISBN 9780062995971 (ebook)
Subjects: CYAC: Wild horses—Fiction. | Captive wild animals—Fiction. | Pony express—Fiction. | West (U.S.)—History—19th century—Fiction. | LCGFT: Animal fiction. | Historical fiction. | Novels.
Classification: LCC PZ7.P248 Ho 2023 | DDC [Fic]—dc22
LC record available at https://lccn.loc.gov/2023020160

23 24 25 26 27 LBC 5 4 3 2 1

First Edition

Greenwillow Books

*To all those who fight for clean air
and water and advocate for creatures
who cannot speak for themselves*

CONTENTS

A HORSE NAMED SKY

CHAPTER ONE

HOME WATERS

My first memory is the sound of water. The warmth of the sun. The smell of my mother. The touch of her tongue on my skin, and the horizon a great circle around me. My second memory is the urge to run. It comes in one breath before I even have the strength to stand. I shake the wet off my mane. Mother licks me from ears to hooves. The wind carries smells sharp and fresh and sweet: piñon trees, sagebrush, and water.

The horses of my family band lift their heads. Turn their

ears toward me. Each auntie holds me in her deep brown gaze. Each one breathes me in.

"He's a small one," Auntie Gale says.

Auntie Rain noses along my legs as if to look for more of me. "He'll get bigger," she says firmly.

Auntie Gale nudges the white splotches on my chestnut coat. "Cloud marked," she says. "Like our stallion."

"May he grow to be a fighter like him," Auntie Rain says.

"We will call you Sky," Mother decides.

The aunties crowd together to block the wind that makes me shiver. But they let the sun shine through to dry me.

"We are your shelter for as long as you grow," Mother says.

"Stay close," says Auntie Rain.

"We will watch for danger," Auntie Gale says.

I take in the sight and smell of my family. Mother's bright chestnut coat. The shining black of Auntie Rain and the rich earth smell of Auntie Gale.

Sagebrush shades my resting place. Golden clumps of grass bend over in the wind. Yellow and brown birds flit from shrub to shrub. I gaze up at the blue curve of sky and pale clouds running, running, running. Already I want to be running like them.

Mother and the aunties browse slowly.

Reach. Bite.

Look to the trees.

Chew. Flick ears forward.

Sniff. Chew.

Look to the horizon. Chew again.

Flick ears to the back.

Turn. Sniff. Check the hillsides.

Reach. Bite.

Our stallion, Thunder, stands on the ridge above, black-and-white against the blue sky. He watches, listens, waits for danger. Burros graze all around him, and farther away, the slender and shy deer. Birds swoop in. Their high voices float on the breeze, but the moment a dark shadow sweeps across the ground, they all go as silent as little brown stones.

A silver shimmer in the valley below catches my eye. The shimmer spreads out like the web of a spider. Bands of horses come to the water to drink in turns. Pronghorn too. All the many scampers come to the water, the big one who catches fish and the tiny ones who hide in burrows. Fiercer creatures come to the water alone, and crowds of swimming birds never leave its ponds and puddles and streams.

"Your home waters," Mother says, looking across the broad valley. "All your strength will come from it."

She comes back to lick me again, firm and steady.

I untangle my legs. Press the front pair deep into the dirt and push until they are straight, and I'm sitting up. A pale gray yearling comes near for a sniff. She gives me a playful nudge that rolls me over onto my back. I blow a frustrated snort at her, and she snorts right back. I work my way to belly down, and she nudges me right over again!

"Storm," Auntie Rain says. "Sky is new. Give him a chance."

Rain's filly is skinny and long legged. She's gray as a moonbeam and bold as a bolt of lightning.

"Back legs first," she says. "Hurry up!"

She springs away from me, races around our mothers, and comes back. I want to run like her so much! I shake my stubby mane and try again. I stretch my front legs out straight and think about the back two.

I bend. Straighten. Push. Wobble.

Mother stands at my side, steadily crunching. Letting me figure it out for myself.

Storm is one long string of advice.

"Push harder!"

"Nope."

"Both legs."

"Bend first and then push."

"That will never work!"

"Try again."

"He's not getting it!"

Mother stays beside me, steady and silent.

Auntie Rain flicks a disapproving ear in Storm's direction.

Auntie Gale presses her lips together hard.

Storm huffs out a disappointed snort. Then she turns and buries her head under Auntie Rain's belly. Suddenly there is the most delicious smell. I don't know what it is, but I want it!

One final heave with the back legs, and they go straight. I sway. Push my legs out wider to steady them. Then I bend my front legs, hooves down, and take a breath.

Push!

My head rises up, level with my rump. Legs shaky but up.

Up!

I look from foot to foot, hardly believing they're holding me. The wind dries my damp skin. I blink against the blowing dust. Auntie Gale inspects me closely. Nudges gently at my hips and shoulders. I try to hold steady, but I wobble at the slightest touch.

"Stay close!" she commands.

"Can't we rest? Just for one day?" Auntie Rain says. "I don't hear danger."

"The howlers will smell it," Auntie Gale says. She looks sternly at a lump of something dark red and sticky on the ground behind Mother. "They'll come with their yipping and yowling. They'll hunt him. You know they will."

"Hush," Mother says softly. She moves closer. I lean against her for balance. "No need to speak of hunters yet."

I don't know what it means to hunt, but I shiver at the sound of it.

Auntie Gale and the stallion move to higher ground, where they can listen in all directions.

I look down at my home waters and then beyond them to where the mountains and sky meet—a frost-white line between the gray and the blue. Though it's far away, I feel the tug of that horizon calling me.

A gruff cry rings out. The shadow of a huge bird races across the ground. Little squeakers nibbling the grass dive for their holes. I duck under Mother's belly.

"The hunter bird does not hunt for you," Mother says.

I shake off the jolt of panic with a toss of my head. I'm hungry. So hungry! Now that I'm standing, the wonderful smell is even closer. I nose along Mother's belly with the sound of her lifebeat in my ears. And then I find it—milk. Better than the best thing I've ever eaten since. I drink until I cannot swallow more.

"I am your first water," Mother says. "And you will always find strength in me."

I breathe in her smell and the

feel of her skin and the sound of her voice and slide to the ground to sleep.

In my dreams I see the gray-blue horizon. In my dreams I can already run toward it. In my dreams I hear the call of the hunting bird. And then I'm awake. Wide-awake. Blinking. Lifebeat racing. Not knowing why.

On the wind comes the sound. *Yip yip ooooooo!*

"Follow!" Mother commands.

I spring to my feet, walking . . . trotting . . . running after her in the moonlight. The aunties and Storm run beside me. Thunder behind and the howlers behind him. We run together under the stars. One band. Safe and strong.

CHAPTER TWO

GROWING UP

We outrun the howlers that first night. We outrun them again the next night. The morning after, the howlers come again, and our stallion turns and fights. After that, the pack moves on.

"Speed is strength," Thunder says to me. "Never fall behind."

The pack doesn't chase us again, but I remember their smell and their snarl and the dying groan of the deer they take instead of me. The deer who is not fast enough.

Don't fall behind is my first thought when I wake. Even in my sleep I listen for Mother calling me to follow.

Storm wakes me most days.

"Let's go!" she says. "Follow me!"

In a whirl of dust she's gone, me sprinting after her. Together we trace the edges of every stream and puddle and pond of the vast wetland that makes up our home waters. We splash into the shallows and scare the fisher birds into the sky on their broad white-and-black wings.

"Look at that!" she says, flushing a scamper out of its hiding place. "Look at this!"

We find a big wrinkly lizard lifting its head and tasting the air. It's basking in the midday sun on a flat-topped rock.

"Bet you can't catch it!" Storm says.

I can never resist her dares. I walk toward the lizard as slowly and quietly as I can. I don't know if a lizard can smell. I'm careful not to let my shadow fall across it. Even so, it guesses I'm coming. The lizard scampers into a crevice between the boulders. I lunge and seize its thick tail in my teeth, but it has already blown up its body to wedge itself in tight. No amount of tugging works it free.

Storm laughs and all the little burros laugh with her, but I can't be mad. Who could guess that a lizard could grow so big in an instant?

Storm moves on to her next bold adventure. One day she picks fights with a badger. The next we race with the yearling burros. She dares us all to jump over streams and tumbleweeds. A willing band of yearlings, horses and burros alike, follow her everywhere. Old Jack, the stallion of the burros, has harsh words for her when she leads us to where he cannot watch over his own. I'm afraid of Old Jack's temper, even though I'm as tall as him by the spring of my first year.

But even in the face of Old Jack's scolding, Storm is fearless. And so fast! I dream of running as fast as her. Season after season, I struggle to catch her. I blink away the dust she kicks up. I stretch my short legs to match hers. I get faster every day, but I never catch her.

I should be practicing my punches and kicks

with the colts of other bands, but they are all so much bigger than me. Speed is my strength.

Long-legged Storm is glad to spar with the colts. She has a spin-kick they never see coming. The mares scold Storm for her bluster, but I adore her and wish I was as bold.

Sometimes Mother takes the band saltward to where the water comes bubbling out of the ground, hot as the sun and bitter to taste. We hunt for salty rocks while our stallion wades into the steaming waters, grumbling about his aches and pains.

When thick black clouds blow in, we climb to the ridgetops and call down the rain and sleet and wind that come from stormward. We lick icicles and dance in the snow. We watch the stars walk from one horizon to the other.

When the warm winds come up from saltward and the frozen ground goes soft, the grasses around our home waters turn yellow and red, pink and purple, white and blue with flowers. Their sweet and sharp smells swirl around us. We listen to every buzzing thing and chase the orange and yellow flutters from one bloom to the next.

"Be careful!" Mother says. "Save your strength."

"Do not eat the purple flowers," Auntie Rain reminds us. "They will make you fall and never get up."

"And watch for the claw beast!" Auntie Gale adds. She nips us both on the rump—but mostly Storm, who is not the listener.

Auntie Gale gives the trees around us a hard stare. While she does, I steal a look at the thick fight marks running side by side down her back. When she was a filly no older than Storm, a claw beast jumped on her. She bucked and spun and kicked until the claw beast let go. Afterward Mother and Auntie Rain stayed by her side night and day. They helped her heal and find her courage. When Auntie Gale cries in her sleep, Mother is always there. When Auntie Gale shivers from nose to tail over a yowling in the night, Auntie Rain is right beside her.

"Sorry, Auntie," I say, giving her neck a nibble.

"I looked! I smelled!" Storm says with an impertinent twitch of the ear. "No claw beast. I promise!"

Auntie Gale snorts at her for being so impulsive, but then she leans in to her. Storm rocks with her as trees do in the wind.

"I will always stay beside you," Storm says.

Auntie Gale heaves a grateful sigh.

I wish I could say the same. It's not a promise a colt can make. Fillies are born to stay with the mares of their family. Colts are meant to move on, whether they want to or not.

But not yet . . . not today.

CHAPTER THREE
ON THE RIDGETOP

Seasons pass, and I become a good runner—almost as fast as Storm. But I'm never as daring or as tall. She climbs ridges. Digs up frogs just to see them churn their tiny back legs until they are covered in gravel again. I think she would pick a fight with the prickly weasel just for the thrill of it. We find new paths. We wake in the dark to watch the night bird fly in complete silence.

Best of all, we find the hidden spots where fresh water comes bubbling out of the ground, cold and delicious. We blow softly upon the water for thanks whenever we find springs. We need them in the dry season, when bears and packs of howlers come to our home waters for relief. We share the water, as all creatures must. But in the dry season, it's good to have hidden waters for refuge. We guard the secret of them.

One summer day when the grasses are fading from green to yellow gray, I run with Storm to the very top of the hills. It takes all morning. We are dusty and sweaty by the time we reach the spine of the hills. But I don't care. From the ridgetop, the whole world spreads out before us. The sunrise side of the ridge has a river, wide and sparkling. It curves through the hills. Humans and their draggers walk along the river. The draggers have thick necks and broad shoulders. Their short antlers go out to the sides instead of up. They drag all manner of odd loads behind them. Usually humans head toward the snow-topped mountains on the sunset horizon. But today, we see humans leave the river and come up

our hill. They set down their loads and stay.

"What do you think they are doing?" I ask.

"They must be here for the trees," Storm says.

In summers past, humans came to our home waters, buckskin-dun humans with black manes. Big ones and little ones together. They took the cones off the piñon trees. Picked them from the ground and from the low branches. They boosted the little ones on their shoulders to pick from higher up. They shook seeds out of the cones. They broke off bits of sage and bundled them together. A few days later they left, carrying the seeds and sage away with them. Nobody knew why they did this. Not Mother, not any of the aunties. Even the burros did not know.

"They always come in the summers," Old Jack told us in that gruff, shouty voice burros have. "Humans do strange things," he added. "None can understand them."

I tried a piñon cone once, in case it was food.

It was not.

The humans coming up our hill today are

not the piñon gatherers.

But they must be here for the trees. What else could it be?

Storm and I keep an eye on them as we hunt for the sweetest flowers. The pink ones that hug the ground are my favorite. Storm likes the spicier yellow ones. Mother and the aunties follow us, keeping pace with Frost, our newest foal. Our stallion tops the ridge and finds his usual place—grass to eat and a view of his whole band. He glares at each treetop where the claw beast might be waiting to pounce. He searches the horizon for roving stallions come to steal the aunties from him. His coat holds many fight marks from all the dangers he's driven away.

Someday soon I will have to fight him. Mother says it has always been this way. The fillies stay and settle. The colts fight or leave.

"Sometimes the colt wins and stays," Storm

likes to remind me. I can't imagine driving our stallion away. One challenger after another has come to fight him—all of them bigger than me. He always wins.

A shiver runs through me at the thought of it. I don't want to fight anybody.

Storm rears up and gives the air a few strikes with her front feet.

If I were danger, I would be afraid of Storm.

The stallion tosses his head to remind her—again—that fillies don't fight. She rears up one more time just to be contrary, then gives me neck nibbles. I close my eyes as she nibbles away my itches and my worries.

"You'll be stronger than him someday," she says.

I rub against her neck in thanks, but I don't believe her. Our stallion is so tall. And he never, never, never gives up. I don't want to leave. I want to stay here by my home waters, with my mother and aunties, with my Storm. But the only way to stay is to fight the stallion and win. To drive him away and take his place.

I will never be that brave. I'm sure of it.

CHAPTER FOUR

PIÑON TREES

All summer long, Storm and I watch the far side of the hills. More humans come every day—red-maned ones and brown and gray. They crowd in like bees in a hollow tree. They move rocks. Dig holes. Entire bands of horses run away from the diggers. They come to our side of the hills. They take a share of our water. For the first time in my life, I wonder if my home waters hold enough for us all.

"Stay away from these humans," Thunder commands. "Don't let them see you." He guards the paths to the ridgetop and nips us when we try to sneak around him.

But Storm and I are much too clever for him. He likes to rest when the sun is high. Mother and the aunties doze too, their heads resting on each other's hips and shoulders. Frost sleeps in their shade. Storm and I pretend to drowse. Sometimes we get sleepy ourselves, to the steady hum of bees and the shush of dry wind through pine needles. But today I give Storm a silent nudge, and we slip away.

We approach the ridgetop carefully. We listen for the odd clangs and sharp brays the diggers make as they work. We see a human walking toward us. A burro follows him. The burro is being pulled along with a line around his neck. I've never seen such a thing.

Old Jack is a fighter. He's every bit as scarred and grouchy as our own stallion. He'd never let a human take one of his own. This must be some lost burro with no family to protect him.

The human stops by a particularly tall and spreading

piñon tree. He swings a stick at the trunk. Birds burst from the branches and whoosh away over the top of the forest. The stick has something on the end of it, something sharp like a tooth or a claw. The human is fighting the tree!

Old Jack is right. There is no understanding humans. Why fight a tree who can't fight back? A tree who has never done you harm? We watch blow after blow land hard and bite deep. With a sickening crack and a burst of sharp smell, the tree falls. The entire thing, as if a great winter storm has toppled it. The human ties the tree to the burro. Together they walk away, dragging the tree behind. It leaves a long fight mark in the dirt.

I've seen things die before: birds and flowers and fish. I've seen the bones of deer and horses gone to the earth, as all of us must go when we grow old. But this killing of a tree—a tree that has done nothing but offer shade and shelter all its long life. I do not understand it.

When the human is gone, Storm and I go to the fallen tree trunk. My lifebeat throbs as though I've been running. The crunch of cones that circle a piñon trunk echo into the newly empty space. Clear, sparkling tree blood oozes down from the broken trunk. I will never forget the smell of it, sharp and bitter like anger.

"Terrible," Storm says.

"Worse than danger," I agree.

We run from that place all the way back to our home waters. But our waters are never the same again.

CHAPTER FIVE

SECRET SPRING

Summer weather goes on and on—even as the days grow shorter. A hot wind blows across my home ground, and I am always thirsty. The bunchgrass grows brittle. Shrubs dry and drop their leaves. The pronghorn move away; the deer become scarce. Waterbirds take to the sky in long, noisy lines, all flying saltward. Streams and pools go dry. Their muddy bottoms crack and crumble and blow away. Those who remain eat sage and hope for rain.

Old Jack is the oldest, the most scarred of all the stallions of my home waters. He has seen hard summers before. Last year in the dry season he said,

"I've seen worse!" He said, "Rains will come."

This year he says, "Enough! We cannot stay." He searches the sky for a turn in the weather. "There is a better place," he says. "A safer place."

He gathers all his jennies together. My burro playmates fall into place with their mothers, and he leads them away.

"Where will you go?" I call after him.

"Stormward," Old Jack says. "An old burro once told of a place where there is a single mountain standing alone. With a swift river, a white salt desert, and none of your troublesome humans."

"How far?" I ask. I try to imagine a single mountain. All the mountains I know stand in a line of brother mountains.

"It doesn't matter how far," Old Jack says. "We must go."

"Go. Go," his jennies mutter. "For the sake of our foals, we must go."

"Before it's too late," Old Jack says. He takes his family stormward in a cloud of kicked-up dust.

The aunties fret about his leaving. They grumble about the crowded watering places. They worry about the winter rains that are late.

"We need new waters," Auntie Gale says firmly.

"Hidden waters," Mother says.

"There's a spring!" Storm sings out. "I remember the way!"

But it's Auntie Gale who leads us. We walk slowly up one ridge and down the next, through the heat of the day. As the sun heads for the horizon, each clump of grass and stone grows a long shadow that points toward where the sun will come up. We pause as we always do to face the setting sun and thank it for light and warmth. We keep going through the rising of the moon and the cold of night and finally the fading of the stars. Little Frost is stumbling with fatigue when we find our secret spring.

It's a seep of water hidden away in the cleft between two ridges. The water bubbles out of the ground and rolls across a broad, speckled stone. A green stripe of shrubs and grass shades the trickle of water. There's only room at the stone for one horse to drink. Rain goes first so she can make milk for Frost. And then Gale and then Mother. Storm comes next, then Frost. The sun is well above the hills when it's finally my turn.

"Thank you," I mutter, as all horses do. I lower my mouth to the stone. I sip and lap and lick. I could have stayed there and kept drinking all day, but our stallion is waiting, and water is meant to be shared.

CHAPTER SIX

THE CHALLENGER

We stay at the spring all day, resting, taking slow sips of water, and hunting for salty rocks to lick. The next day is hotter and drier. We stay. The day after that is hot and dry and windy. The winter stars are rising, but the winter rains have not come.

"Has the rain ever been so late?" Storm asks.

"Never," Auntie Gale says.

The mares grow quiet—even Storm. They stand in the shade and eat sage, slowly and patiently. Frost whimpers for milk, and the stallion grumbles against our rough luck. He chases me away from the water so the mares can drink. Someday he will drive me away forever. And if the rain doesn't fall, that day will come soon.

I try not to complain. I move less so that I will need less. I distract Frost with the stick game. I give Mother soothing neck nibbles. I help watch over the band.

I'm the first one to see a buckskin-dun stallion come into the ravine. His nostrils go wide, and he gives a nicker of relief at the scent of water. The old stallion stands between the newcomer and the spring.

"There isn't enough," Thunder says. "Find your own."

I feel a chill clear down to my hooves. Water is for sharing—but in the dry times a stallion must fight for his band's water.

I take a step forward to stand beside our stallion—to defend our band together. Mother turns me aside with a sharp look.

"Save your strength," she says. "You will need all of it for yourself."

The dun arches his neck and makes a big smelly pile. He throws a few punches at the air. Thunder stands his ground. Dumps a pile of his own. Gives the intruder an angry stare. Then he holds completely still. I've seen this trick before. Our stallion likes to stall a fight until the younger stallion comes to doubt Thunder's strength and relaxes his guard.

I watch and wait. I want the young stallion gone. I want all the water for my own band. But I know my time will come. Maybe very soon. If I'm going to stay, I need to learn how to fight our stallion and win.

The buckskin dun chooses the spin-kick. A tactic that favors a young horse with sturdy legs. But Thunder is tall. He lifts his head clear and lets the blows fall on his chest where his muscles are thick. The dun needs a better move to win.

Storm watches every turn of the fight, restless, longing to land a blow of her own. The mares stand apart, tight-lipped and watchful.

Our stallion has won more battles than there are stars in the sky. He has the aches and fight marks to prove it. But what if he loses? We are so thirsty. We have this one spring to defend. Even mares fight in the dry season.

The dun paces. Shows his teeth. Tries his spin-kick again. Thunder waits for his moment. He doesn't waste energy on a blow he can't land.

Storm loses her patience. She steps out of the shade. Her silver coat gleams in the sun like a pool of clear water. She turns to face the dun. Her white mane ripples in the wind. She holds her tail high and nickers softly.

The young stallion steals a glance her way.

In a flash Thunder rears up, steps forward, and comes down with all his weight over the shoulders of the upstart. A better fighter would have guessed this move was coming. A better fighter would have dodged away, leaving Thunder to come down hard on empty air and feel that landing in every one of his creaky old knees.

But the youngster falls under the weight of our stallion. I wince in sympathy as he staggers to his feet, shakes off shame, and trots away.

"Well done," Storm murmurs, as she returns to her spot in the shade.

"Bravely fought," the mares say.

"You are going to lead us all one day," I tell Storm.

Clearly this is the hidden secret to victory—a true-hearted friend. What could I ever do to deserve a companion as brave and true as Storm? I will never find another like her.

Our stallion is thirsty after his fight. He takes a long drink from the spring. The mares drink next. As it should be. By the time I come to the seep, the stone is barely damp. The grasses around the spring have faded from green to gold. And where there was once soft mud that attracted clouds of white and blue flutters, now only cracked dirt remains.

I lower my head to the spring. I breathe out my gratitude as gently as I can. I lick and wait. Little by little the water bubbles up. I glance at Mother and the aunties eating the last of the grass. Tomorrow it will be gone. We should move on. Our way to thank the water for giving us food is to always move on. But where could we go? Nothing but rain will save us.

I nuzzle my mother for comfort. She's getting lean and bony. We all are. The stallion should drive me out. He should do it today. If I go, there will be more water for the mares. More for Frost and Storm.

But Thunder is exhausted from his fight. Worn out from too many days with too little to drink.

I could fight him now. I have a chance in the heat of the day. I know which knee gives him trouble. One low kick, and he would go down.

I chew sage. I think.

I don't want to fight. I only want to stay.

Thunder can defend them all better than I can. Maybe someday I will be big enough to lead them, but I am not that strong today.

I have to do what is best for us all.

Even when it's not what I want.

"I'll go now," I whisper to Mother. "I must."

"It's time," she agrees. She puts her head beside mine and breathes in deeply. "I will never forget you, my bright Sky."

I breathe in and fold the memory of her smell deep inside me. I go to Rain and Gale and Frost and do the same.

Storm waits apart from the others. She gives me neck nibbles. I blow on her ears.

"Don't go," Storm says. "All we need is rain."

I wish it was true. I want it to be true. But colts are made for leaving. Whether we want to or not.

CHAPTER SEVEN

CHASING RAIN

I turn and walk away from the water, from my family, from Storm. Every time I look back, she is still watching me.

I follow the ridgetop all day. When the heat gets fierce, I find a piñon tree and stand in its shade. I doze with the sharp smell of pine around me. I wake and scratch my neck and shoulders against the rough trunk. I keep walking. As the heat rises, dark clouds shadow the horizon. The wind whistles through the sage and runs its cool feathers along my back. Clusters of dry grass bend. Drop seeds. Sway back into place. I breathe in storm smell. The clouds spread. Their bottom edges go flat and black.

"Come on, rain!" I call.

A boom of thunder rolls toward me. The almost-rain smell crackles in the air. Cloud shadows swoop up the ridge.

The rain will come, I promise myself. The tender grasses will grow again. The gullies will swell with water and rush down the hillsides. Just as they did last year and the year before that. Another great roll of thunder rumbles through the hills. A dazzle of lightning zigzags from cloud to cloud.

I reach for the sky with my hooves. I call the rain down with my whole body. It feels so close! Lightning leaps across the sky; thunder right at its heel. I shiver with anticipation.

Rain is falling on the sunup horizon, thick gray lines of it, falling from cloud to ground.

"Come on, sweet rain," I say.

Another crack of lighting. Closer. I smell the burned air. Thunder trembles the ground.

But still no rain.

I cannot wait a moment longer. I run toward the storm. My head throbs from thirst. My tongue feels like sand. But the more I run, the farther away the rain is. In the end, even a storm grows weary; by sundown it's gone. I keep going across the steppe.

I try not to think of my family. Colts like me are made to chase the horizon. But every step brings them to mind. Mother, my aunties, Frost and Storm. Most of all Storm. I've followed her all my life. She chose the direction we would run. She planned the games we played. I followed. Now every time I crest a rise, I look for her.

I have never been alone in the dark before. I slow

to a walk so I don't stumble. Every sudden noise makes my lifebeat race. I don't dare close my eyes or stop to rest.

By sunup I am exhausted. I come at last to the spot where it rained yesterday. The hungry dust has swallowed every drop. But sage keeps water hidden away in her narrow gray leaves. I go from one sagebrush to the next, licking up every precious drop. It's not nearly enough, but the smell of wet sage gives me hope.

I've never tried to find water on my own before. I search all day and see nothing but dirt, bunchgrass, sage, and rocks. I walk. Browse. Rest. A crowd of birds, blue gray and noisy, keep me company, flitting from shrub to tree. They give their songs to the wind without a care. Maybe sorrow has no hold on a creature who can fly.

The next day I'm fuzzy-headed with thirst. I kick a tuft of grass. Blow out my frustration.

After much thought I say, "Water goes from up to down," to the long-eared bounder who races across the ground. It freezes midhop when it catches sight of me.

I turn my ears its way, but it offers nothing about hidden streams or secret springs. Bounders are the wrong folk to ask. They don't come to the water, as all who run on hooves do.

Water likes a ravine better than a ridge, I remember.

"I should go down into the ravines to look for it," I say to the air around me. My ears turn from front to back, and a nervous twitch runs up my legs. A ravine, with its overhanging rocks, makes a perfect hiding spot for a claw beast. They wait up there with their teeth and their bloodthirsty thoughts. A horse alone is easy to kill.

I take a mouthful of sage and consider my options. A bee zooms along, looking for flowers. It's better if you don't eat the bees. They have a sharp on one end that hits you like a kick in the teeth. I watch the bee zip from stalk to shrub. Their rule about flowers must be the same as our rule about water—take what you need and move on.

"Water makes a sound," I tell the bee. "I could hear it better from a ridgetop—where the claw beast does not like to go."

"And water has a smell," I remember aloud. "It makes things green, which I could see if I was up."

I set out for higher ground.

All day I walk along the ridge. I keep one eye and ear firmly on the ground so I don't step on a slither. I give every rocky outcropping a good stare, looking for the golden fur of a claw beast, the black-rimmed eyes, the long tail with the black tip. I go down one ravine and up the next ridge. A band of pronghorn browse in the distance. There's not a tree or a scrap of shade anywhere. Heat shimmers flicker. From the next ridge I see a ravine with a pale swoosh of green down the middle. The wind carries the faintest smell of fresh grass.

I move closer.

Watch for trouble.

Listen for danger.

The nearer I get, the louder the water sounds. When I finally reach the ravine, I scramble down to the stream—so thirsty I forget to look for trouble. I drink and drink until I can feel my belly stretch. I stroll along the stream, pulling up mouthfuls of grass. The rush of sweetness makes me kick up my heels.

And then I hear a clatter of pebbles fall from the rocks above. I spin away, clear the stream in one bound, and scramble up the opposite slope. I throw a glance over my shoulder. A pale shape stands on the far side. I turn away to run.

"Stop! Wait!" a familiar voice calls to me.

I freeze.

"Storm? Is it you?"

"Of course it's me," she says.

I run back down, jump the stream, and sprint to the top of the slope. I rear up just for the joy of seeing her. Storm runs her cheek along my neck. She rests her head on my shoulder. I sigh with relief.

"You left?" I ask. "Mares don't leave."

"A mare can choose," Storm says.

"And you chose . . ." I don't dare say it. Has Storm chosen me? Me? Who has not defeated our stallion?

"There's not enough water," Storm says. "They'll have a better chance now. Frost and Gale, all of them."

I think of Mother. Maybe I should have fought the stallion and brought them all here.

Storm gives me a comforting nudge. "I knew you would find water," she says. "I told them you would. And see, you have!"

I perk up at that. "Yes! I followed my nose and—"

"Drink up," Storm says, taking charge as usual. "And let's find a more open place where we can rest without so many danger spots."

We drink our fill. Storm leads me out of the ravine and onto open ground. We stand together hip to shoulder, each watching for the other. The last light of the day falls on our shoulders, and we turn to the sun with gratitude for so much more than light. We doze and wake in the warmth of each other as the stars travel across the sky. I hope all my days will be like this one, just Storm and Sky, finding our way. Together.

CHAPTER EIGHT

CAPTURE

In the morning, Storm and I head downstream. As the day warms up, we're glad to have water nearby. There is fresh grass along the bank, but only a few steps away the ground is brown and dead. We eat as we go.

Walk.

Browse.

Rest.

By midday, clouds gather on the stormward horizon. The promise of rain blows our way.

"I could go for some salt," Storm says.

We look for the yellow-green saltbush that grows on open ground. We taste the wind for a scent of it.

Storm and I can go anywhere. Anywhere! Yesterday I saw places I've never seen before. Today we could find someplace completely new. Tomorrow anything could happen. Just the thought gives me a shiver of joy.

We are so intent on salt that we don't see the tracks at first. But soon there are too many to ignore—horse tracks, and pronghorn tracks too. I take a closer look. In the middle of them is the oddest rock I've ever seen. It's flat as a pond on top and just as flat on all the sides.

"What's this?" Storm asks.

"Odd-looking rock," I reply.

I watch it from many steps back to make sure it's really a rock. Storm sniffs. She taps it with her hoof.

"It smells familiar," Storm says. She gives it a lick. "Salt!"

"It doesn't look like any salty rock I've ever seen before," I say, still hanging back.

"Who cares?" Storm says. "It's salty."

We settle in for a good lick.

Before long we feel the ground move. I turn my ears to each horizon. Three horses walk toward us. They snort and stomp and play as they come. They are a band of brother stallions. When they get close, we step back. Salt is for sharing, like water. No horse—no matter how big—has the right to take it all.

Two of the brothers are bays with white star marks on their rumps, and one is pale like Storm, with chestnut speckles all over him. They jostle and nip each other, but in the end, the one with the most fight marks licks first. When he's done, he edges closer to Storm, tossing his head for attention.

A crack like lightning bursts out from a clump of shrubs in the distance. We spin toward the sound. A yip-yowl like a whole pack of howlers comes from the shrubs. Horses charge out of them and head straight for us. Humans sit on their backs, riding them like a claw beast would.

"Run!" the speckled horse shouts. He whirls away from me and Storm and sprints for the horizon. His brothers follow.

The humans on horses sweep across the steppe like fire. I turn and run, Storm right beside me. I rock my neck forward and back with each stride. Tail straight out behind me. Eyes darting ahead and behind, looking for the rock or ditch that will break my stride. We catch up to the brothers and pull ahead. The horses and humans draw closer. They are tall and fast. The humans haven't killed them as the claw beast does. No bitten necks. No claws sunk deep into their backs.

"Dodge!" Storm calls. She swerves to the side.

I veer in the opposite direction. The brothers charge straight ahead. One of the riders follows me, pouring on speed. He cuts me off. I turn back to the middle. The horses from the brother band run close beside me.

"Too many to fight," their leader pants.

"Speed will save us," I say.

And for a while it does. We turn as a group one way and then the other. We are faster than the riders. But they keep coming.

They are heavier than us and breathing hard.

"We can outlast them!" I shout.

"Follow me!" Storm says.

Ahead is a canyon. It will slow us down, but we can find a way to climb up the steep side. A way that the bigger horses can't follow.

I pour on the speed. Following Storm. The brother band falls in behind me.

Running together. Breathing together. Flying together.

I could run forever!

We enter the canyon. The sound of our hooves

echoes on the rocks. We slow just enough to search for a path up and out. The sides of the canyon seem to lean in, offering us shade but no escape.

The riders charge into the canyon after us.

Hard and flat ground lies ahead, with hardly any sagebrush to dodge around.

Strange.

The canyon walls curve and narrow.

"Dead end!" Storm calls.

"Turn around!" I shout.

We turn, but the sides of the canyon stand like cliffs around us.

"Danger! Danger!" the brothers call.

The humans yip and yowl. They form a line to block our escape. I frantically search the cliff face for a way out of the canyon.

"We can get past them," Storm calls.

"Run hard!" yell the brothers.

I turn sharp, muscles straining.

The riders are before me, and Storm is at my side. I put my head down and charge, dodging between them. Storm and I break through their line. My lifebeat pounds like thunder. Some of them charge past me, still chasing the brother band, but one turns. Soon it's running right beside me. The canyon mouth and open ground lie ahead. The horizon lies ahead. I've never run so far or so fast. I call on the wind to give me speed. I flare my nostrils wide for more breath. Speed is my only hope.

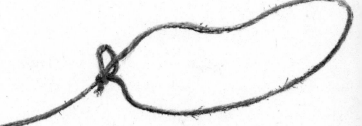

I pull ahead. *Yes!* I fix my eyes on the horizon. *Freedom is so close!*

A thing flies over my head. Low over my head.

A long thin thing.

In the blink of an eye, it slides over my ears. Down my nose.

Tight around my neck.

Around my neck!

I shake my head to be free of it, but it grows tighter.

I gasp for air. It pulls me back. Strong like a flowing river.

"Stop!" I cry. "Let me go!"

I shake my head. The pull digs in like a claw.

The horse behind me slows.

I slow.

I refuse to stop. I refuse to be eaten! I keep running, but slower. My legs shake; I gasp for air.

The horse behind me stops.

The pull cuts deep.

My front legs go up. Up. Up. And over.

I come down hard on my back.

The thing around my neck goes straight to the
horse and rider. I scramble to my feet, shaking. I face
them. I tug the line. They don't move.

"Let me go!"

"They never let us go," the horse says.

I back away. Look for Storm. The horse is taller
than me and black as a moonless night.
But he doesn't have the fight marks of
a lead stallion. Maybe he doesn't
know how to fight. Maybe I can
fight him and win. I kick in
his direction. I rear up. The
black horse stands firm.

"Fighting will
bring you pain,"
he says.

"No!"

"They will
never let you go."

"How can you stand a creature—that creature—on your back—like a claw beast!"

He takes a step closer.

"There will be food," he says.

"I can find my own food," I snort.

"There will be water."

I blow out an angry breath. Water is harder to find on my own than I thought.

The black horse comes toward me. I step back. He turns, and the line between us grows shorter. He walks and pulls me alongside.

I follow him back to the canyon. The brother band is bunched together, still struggling for a way out—Storm is with them. Canyon walls block our escape.

"Settle," the black horse says. "Give up."

Storm and the brothers turn and push and stumble. Frightened. Angry. I cannot save them. Danger is on all sides, and there is no place to run.

CHAPTER NINE

THE CANYON

The humans drag branches across the canyon opening. They go back for more, stacking them tall to make a trap. They take off my line.

Storm searches the canyon walls for footholds or a hidden path. The cliffs are sheer and straight. We run the small circle of our trap, panic rising. A dry wind blows through the canyon. There is no horizon. Only a stripe of sky above us, turning from pale blue to amber.

The humans get off the horses. They stand on their back legs and lean against the barrier. They point at us with their front legs and chatter like blackbirds. The ridden horses stay off to the side, heads down, eating. They have some kind of trap around their bodies. A strap goes under their bellies. A thick lump sits on their backs where the humans perched. Lines go round their mouths and heads and down their necks.

"What should we do?" one of the brothers says.

"Where will we go?" another asks.

They turn to Storm as if she's a lead mare already.

"Steady," she says to them firmly. "Save your strength." She blows out her fears. She draws in a breath of calm.

There's no food, I think. *And no water.* I don't say those things aloud. I force my feet to stop running. I blow out my fears too, but my next breath holds not one scrap of hope.

"But the claw beast," the speckled brother says, searching along the rim of the canyon. "One could drop on us at any moment."

The black horse snorts in disdain. "Fear not," he says. "The claw beast runs from humans."

"Humans are small," says another of the ridden

horses. "But they are powerful."

Storm comes to my side. She tosses her mane boldly, and I take in her courage.

The humans take the perches off the horses but leave the lines around their heads. One by one, they are taken away to drink, and brought back. I can smell the water on their skin when they return. I can feel it in their contentment.

No water comes our way.

The humans spark a fire in their circle. But instead of spreading out in a line of flame and burning up the grass with the speed of the wind, this fire stays in the circle of humans. Sparks fly up, and smoke, but it never runs away from them.

Who are these creatures to control even fire— the most powerful thing of all?

My anger grows. *I cannot let them have Storm. Not my Storm!*

She followed me. She trusted me.

We have to escape!

I will find a way.

At moonrise, the humans lie on the ground and make the heavy breath of sleep. I check the branches that block the end of the trap. They are stacked but not held fast. I could push them down if I had help. Not all of them. But enough to jump.

We make a plan. We wait while the silver eye of the moon passes over the rim of the canyon, spilling its light down on us. In time the moon moves on, and the canyon bottom falls into shadow.

I go to the weakest part of the barrier. The others line up with me. I kick the branches hard with my back legs. Storm and the brothers do the same. The crack of our hooves meeting wood echoes down the canyon. Branches break free and roll off the top of the stack. The humans wake up. Storm runs once around

the circle
of our trap,
gaining speed.
I kick the barrier
again. Another
branch falls.

"Go!" I call to Storm.

She puts on a burst of
speed. Lifts her front legs. Pushes hard with the
back ones. She clears the barrier, and I pause a fatal
moment to admire her strength.

"Follow!" she calls as she runs out of the canyon.
"Follow! Follow!"

The brothers are right behind her. One clears
the barrier easily. The other takes a blow to the shin
before landing outside the trap.

The humans leap to their feet, shouting. One
rides off after Storm and the escaping brothers.

The speckled stallion jumps and misses. He falls
hard in front of me. I dodge him and circle around
again to take the jump. The fire blazes up. Humans

stand all along the barrier with flaming sticks in their hands. I rear up instead of jumping. I see Storm and the two brothers reach the mouth of the canyon and then disappear into the darkness.

The one who fell and blocked my escape scrambles roughly to his feet. He winces in pain and struggles hard to not show a limp. I watch the darkness where I last saw Storm.

"Wind run beside her," I whisper to the stars. "Give her speed and carry her far, far away."

At sunrise the humans who chased her come back alone.

"She's free!" I say to the speckled stallion.

"What a jumper!" he says. "And a beauty." He rocks slowly, favoring his bruised leg. "She's a brave one, like my brothers. Wind run beside them."

My sorrow is too heavy to speak. I could say all that and more in her praise. Without Storm, all my horizons feel empty.

CHAPTER TEN

ANTHILL

I promise the wind I will never give up.

I swear to the stars I will escape.

But for days the speckled stallion and I do nothing at all. At first our heads are high, watching every twitch of movement from the humans, listening to every chirp and scurry, sniffing the air for some hint of what is coming. But nothing happens.

The sun makes its daily gallop across the sky. The speckled stallion tells me he left his band a few seasons ago. They called him Fire for the marks scattered across his white coat, like sparks from a burning tree. I thought he would want to spar with me, as brother stallions do. But he only wants to be free.

"I should never have left the Alone Mountain," Fire says. "We had everything: water, salt, room to run, and none of these . . . creatures." He glances at the humans.

"Did your stallion drive you away?" I ask.

He blows out hard against that bitter memory. Fire is so much taller than I am, but his stallion ran him off just the same. What hope is there for me?

"And you?" Fire says. "You must be stronger than you look if Storm left the mares of her band for you."

"We're strong together," I say. I tell him all about my home waters and my band. About the humans who came and the rains that did not.

As the days pass, most of the humans and horses leave. Only the black horse and his rider stay. We get hungrier. Thirstier. There is food and water each day for the black horse, but none for us. We comfort each other with neck nibbles and stories of home.

In the end, we hold still. Heads low.

We hope for food and water.

We know it will never come.

One morning, when blackbirds are making noisy circles above the canyon, the human comes into the trap. He holds a carrier like the piñon gatherers use to carry away pine nuts. But this one is full of water. I can smell it. I breathe in as if I could drink through my nose. The human puts his grabber in the water and holds it out to me. I can hear each drop fall like the first promise of rain. I take a step toward him.

Even the mightiest of us is only as strong as our last drink of water.

I lick from the human's grabbers, and he puts a line around my neck. I don't fight. I want to. But I barely have the strength to stand. I lower my head into the water carrier and drink it dry. And then the human opens the trap and pulls me over to the black horse.

"The human always wins," the black says. "Fighting will only bring you pain."

He is covered in human smell. The human is always touching him. The lines around his head have a hard jangly piece that goes right through his mouth. I shudder at the sight of it.

"It will go better now," the black horse says. "Follow, and they will not hurt you."

The human ties me to the black, who looks fast even with all the things he carries.

"If we run away together, they'll never catch us," I say. "I'll take you to my home waters, and you'll be free."

He stomps his foot hard against my plan. "You'll never get *this* if we run," he says. He motions to a sack on the ground. It's full of the sweetest-smelling . . . something.

Not grass.

Not shrubs.

The black horse moves his head to the side, inviting me in. I take a lick. A mouthful of thick crunchy bits like the seeds of grass goes down before I can even think about whether it's safe to eat.

Mother always told me to try a little bit of a new plant and then wait to see if it made me sick. But I can't wait. I gulp down another mouthful of the crunchy bits, and then another. Nothing has ever tasted so good—or left me feeling so hollow.

Soon Fire is caught and tied behind me. We head out of the canyon like a pair of foals following our mother. We walk all day. It didn't rain once while we were in the trap. The steppe is even more dry than before. We find a few streams to drink from, but they are warm and low. No matter how tall the grass or how savory the shrubs or how much I tug at him to stop and eat, the black horse keeps walking. He doesn't browse once.

Shadows grow long, and still we walk, up one hill and down another. As soon as I have the strength, I will run away. But today I'm as shaky as a newborn foal. I watch for the signs and smells that will lead me home when I do escape.

We keep going by moonlight. My sole comfort is knowing that Storm is running free. We pause to doze just once, and I dream of my home waters. The human keeps us tied to the black horse even when we are asleep.

"Come with me," I whisper to him. "If we run together, they will never ride you again."

The black snorts loudly against that plan, and the human rolls over and opens his eyes.

My hope for freedom fades away like stars do in the morning.

🔥 🔥 🔥

The next day we come to a huge anthill of humans. Rows of dirt-colored blocks stand on each side of a square field. Humans walk in lines across the field, one beside the next, like birds in the sky. They walk from one block to another, going inside and coming out again. Beyond the blocks are horses penned up in a big trap. A smaller empty trap lies beside it. Beyond the horses there's a stand of tall, tall trees with leaves flickering in the wind. Only a river can birth trees so tall.

Fire and I follow the black horse and rider. The other humans pay no attention to us but keep walking in their lines. Old Jack is right. There's no sense at all in the things humans do.

We are taken to a long box filled with water. We dip our heads in and drink our fill. Afterward they lead us into the smaller trap and untie us. I rear up, shaking my head from side to side, grateful to be able to move as I choose. Fire and I run along the edges of the trap, but the humans close the gate. No amount of pushing with my head or shoulders will open it.

"Where are we?" Fire says. "What will happen to us?"

All the horses in the larger trap next to ours are black or dark bay with black manes. We watch the new band carefully. There are no foals or yearlings among them, so no way to tell who's a lead mare. There is no fight-marked older male—the obvious choice for stallion of the band. The horses stand together, blinking against the sun. They swish away the flies, but there's no sparring, not even any teasing or playing.

Odd.

After a while, a mule comes by, dragging a cart loaded with bundles of dry grass. A human tosses a bundle into the larger trap. The horses crowd together to eat. They do not take turns. Nobody stands watch.

Very strange.

A smaller bundle is tossed our way. Fire and I hustle over to eat. We are weak and weary from our time in the canyon. But still we take turns and watch for danger while we try to make up for the days without food. I listen to the chirps and squawks of humans. I see that although the humans have many colors of mane, they all have the same night-sky color wrapped around their skins.

A human goes into the larger trap. At the sight of him, the other horses dodge away like I would from a slither. He flicks a bendy stick at the rump of the horse nearest to him, and the horse jumps as if stung by a bee. The human shouts and prods and pressures with the stick until all the horses are standing in one corner, quivering with anxiety but not trying to run away.

"Look at that," I say to Fire. "That human with the stick is their stallion."

CHAPTER ELEVEN

FIRE STICK

The humans in this new place surround us. Their bustle and clatter and odd smells come at us from all sides. But Fire and I can't take our eyes off the human and the horses in the bigger trap. A human puts a line around each horse's head and leads him to a long, low block that's as dark as a cave inside. Once they're in, I can't even smell them. I can't guess what terrors lurk there. They won't be able to see the horizon or know where danger is coming from.

One of the horses is taken to a post and tied to it.

"Look out!" I call to him.

The horse doesn't flinch as the human approaches.

I watch for the kick. I tense my own muscles, ready for him to land a blow. He tosses his head as if nothing bad is happening.

"Danger!" I shout.

The human rubs him all over. The horse lets it happen. Sighs even, as if he is getting a playful nibble or a soothing nudge. And then, to make matters worse, the human picks up the horse's foot and holds it in his grabber. Still the horse does nothing to fight back.

Baffling!

"We must get away," I say to Fire.

"So many humans," my brother says with a nervous swish of his tail.

"Maybe later," I say, scanning the ground for the best escape route. "After they sleep."

"Come nightfall," he agrees.

One of the humans kindles a fire in a ring of stones. I move away from it, but I can still smell the smoke and hear the crackle. The human puts a long, straight stick into the fire. It's too straight to be a branch. And it doesn't burn like a branch; it only turns orange like the embers that live deep in a log after the flames are gone.

Fire and I stand hip to shoulder to keep watch, but when the human comes for me, there is nowhere to run. The human takes my line and pulls my head forward. I rear up and punch at him. He dodges to the side. I snort in anger and yank against his pull. The human yanks back. I drop my ears and give the human my fiercest stare.

"I'm no colt of yours!" I shout. "Who are you to command me?"

The human keeps pulling my head. I stretch my neck forward, but do not take a step his way. He is persistent, but I am heavier. Just when the human looks ready to give up, I take one step forward and give him my best spin-kick.

If he'd been a horse, I'd have landed a solid

blow. But humans are bendy creatures, and they can hop about like a bird. My kick falls on open air. I rear up again, but another human throws a second line over my head. Together they pull me to a corner of the trap. I tug and kick, but they open the gate and press the rails of it against my side so that I'm held still between them.

I flick my ears forward and back. All around me are sounds I've never heard before. The smoke from the fire drifts my way, and I can't run from it.

"Run!" I say to my brother. "Run now!"

He makes a dash for the open gate, but humans are there with front legs waving. He circles round to jump, but the trap is too small. He rams into the rails. All his strength is not enough to break them down.

A human comes toward me with a stick. It has an orange glow on the end.

"No!" I shout. "Stop!"

The humans hold me fast between the rails. They press the stick into my shoulder, and at first I feel nothing. A cloud of bitter-smelling smoke blows over me and then—oh, the pain!

The burning!

Harder and deeper than any bite.

I kick and scream.

In the blink of an eye, it's over. The humans let me go. I sprint to the far corner of the trap—legs shaking. I swing my head around to look at the raised edges of the wound. It doesn't bleed like a bite. And in truth it doesn't hurt like a bite does, long after the teeth are gone. But the memory of the pain will never leave me.

That's not the worst of it.

My brother is taken to be bitten by the fire stick. Bitten right in front of me. Nothing I can do will save him. I can see what I couldn't see before. I can smell his fear. Feel his panic coursing through my own body. As the fire stick draws near him, I feel the pain anew. The pain and the shame of not protecting him—not breaking out of the trap and running for the horizon. I close my eyes, but I can't shut out the sound of my brother crying out in pain. And after it's done, the bitter smell of burning hangs in the air.

As for what came next, Mother would have cautioned me against it. "Be careful," she'd have said. "Save your strength."

I want to run. I want to race for the horizon and never look back.

But there's no way out. So I do what Thunder would do. Not what he told me, for he said little. But what he lived for and what he one day would die for.

Defend your band. Whatever the cost.

And so when the next human comes into the trap—comes in with a dark stone attached to a stick—grasps my brother by the foot and holds it fast—takes the stone stick and strikes him hard on the sole of his hoof—I do not wait!

I am not careful.

I do what a stallion must for his band. I push the human down. I take his grabber in my mouth. I bite down hard until I hear the crackle of breaking bones.

I am not sorry; I would do it again.

CHAPTER TWELVE

FLAPPY THINGS

After I break the human's grabber, after he flaps and squawks like a bird, after another human takes him by the shoulders and leads him out of the trap—everyone leaves us alone.

All that day and through the night, Fire and I stand shoulder to shoulder. We rock together for comfort. I tell him the waymarks to my home waters, and he tells me the way to the Alone Mountain. It's not the pain that has me wakeful.

I ache from being marked. Marked in a way that no amount of rolling in the dust or standing in the rain will wash away. I ache from knowing I'm not free.

In the morning, a human in a brown wrapper with a broad head cover comes to the trap. His horse is a red roan mare with a burn mark the same as mine. The new human ties me to the mare.

Only me.

He leaves Fire behind.

"Wait," Fire calls. "Don't go!"

The red roan starts to walk, but I dig in to stay beside Fire. The red roan pulls. She's big enough to drag me whether I want to go or not. I can't win, but I can make her fight for every step.

The rider makes a chirp sound. The red roan stomps against my stubbornness.

"Go where the humans take you, and you'll never be thirsty again," she says.

The human opens the trap and leads me out. The horizon lies ahead. With it comes a spark of hope and maybe a chance to escape. It will be much easier to escape on open ground.

Fire sees my chance.

"Go," he says. "Run the moment they're not looking."

He's right, but I hesitate.

"I'll escape too," Fire says. "I promise."

I follow the red roan out of the trap. My brother calls my name as I walk away. I look over my shoulder again and again. Each time he's smaller, until I cannot see him and all the noise of that place is far behind us.

"Who are you?" I say to the red roan, as we take to the hills.

"My own called me Cloud," she says.

"Sky," I answer. "Mine call me Sky."

We turn toward the sunset horizon.

"Are we going to your home waters?" I ask.

Cloud goes quiet as we plod across the sagebrush steppe.

"I haven't seen my home waters in a long time," she says at last. "I could never find my way now."

I resolve to be alert for every landmark and smell mark, so that I can retrace my steps and find my family again.

"You're not very tall," Cloud says. "But you do have the look of a runner. Are you fast?"

"I won't fall behind," I say.

Cloud gives an approving nicker. "This human will be kind to you if you can run."

The morning has a chill in the air. The rains will come soon. They must. Soon the days will grow even shorter and tiny ice flowers will cling to every stalk and branch, and my home waters will get a rim of ice.

The man in the brown wrapper makes a chirping sound like the little striped fellows make when they've found a nut.

"The chirp means go," Cloud says.

"They can talk?"

I cut a glance at the human. He has a white-and-black mane, and his face is wrinkly as a lizard and still as stone. He doesn't move his ears once. Or toss his mane. Or point with his lips. He does not blow against the bad things or breathe gently upon the good.

"Simple phrases," Cloud says. "Try not to confuse them."

The human chirps again. He leans forward on the perch. Cloud moves from a walk to a trot and into an easy lope. A pace to cover ground without getting out of breath. The human's brown wrapper flaps in the wind. I dodge away from the flapping like you would turn away from a hawk that was swooping down on a rabbit.

"Stop that!" Cloud snorts. "It's only the warmer a human puts over his skin. They wear a great many wrappers of all kinds. They do flap about in a way I don't like. But listen here, no horse has ever been attacked or eaten or even nibbled by the wrappers that humans wear."

"Don't like a flappy thing," I say firmly.

"You'll get used to it," Cloud says.

I'll escape and never think about humans and their flappy things again, I say to myself. I fall into step with Cloud. It's good to run. Good to have a horizon on all sides.

When we stop at the river for water, the mare drinks first. The human touches my shoulder as we wait our turn. I shy away from him. I look around for the best path to escape. When it's my turn to drink, the human will untie me and then . . . freedom!

"He means you no harm," Cloud says, water dripping from her chin.

I don't believe her.

Still, the human doesn't bite me. Or kick. I don't know how a human would kick with any force when it only puts two legs on the ground and has the front two dangling uselessly in the air. The human pats me again. I try to hold still, but my skin twitches.

Cloud makes room for me at the water, but the human leaves me tied. I glare at him.

"Go on," Cloud says. She plants her feet firmly on the bank while I drink, and no matter how hard I tug I cannot break away.

We travel on, and when the sun is at the top of the sky, the human stops beside a patch of grass and lets us eat. The grass is hard and dry, but the seed heads are plump and tasty.

The human unties a thing from behind his perch. It's gray and round like a log. He brings it over and lets me look at it, and then he unrolls it.

Another flappy thing!

I hate flappy things.

I turn to the human and say, as clearly as I can, "I. Do not want. That thing!"

He doesn't answer me. I'm not at all sure that Cloud is right about humans being able to talk. The human tosses that gray flappy thing right over my back!

"I said *no*!" I shout at him. I rear up as far as the line will let me. There's no room to kick, so I step on his foot. Only, the human hops away before I can get him.

Humans are bendy in the middle and faster than they look. For such skinny and clawless creatures, humans are not as easy to frighten as you'd think.

"It's a warmer," Cloud says, glaring at me. "There's not a tooth or a claw on it. I promise."

I wear the gray warmer for the rest of the day. It gets colder and darker as the afternoon storm clouds gather. But the wind doesn't chill me. After a while the human gets out a pouch of the sweet-smelling crunchy bits. But instead of letting me eat from the pouch, he dips his own grabbers in and holds some out to me. The sour smell of the human's grabbers is too much. I dodge away.

"You'll get hungry," Cloud says, as she carefully licks the grabbers clean.

She's right. I do get hungry. The wind grows colder, and the way grows steeper. I test the line holding me to Cloud. I'm not strong enough to break it.

"Suppose you do escape," Cloud says. "You're a marked horse now, just like me."

I shudder all over, remembering the fire stick and the smell of burning. "What does it mean to be marked?" I ask.

"The humans are your band now," she says. "No matter how far you run, any human who finds you will bring you back."

"No," I whisper.

"You would not be the first to try," Cloud says gently. "But you will not succeed. No horse does."

All hope of escape dies in me. I turn my face to the setting sun, but I cannot find gratitude, even for light, when my own horizons feel forever dark.

CHAPTER THIRTEEN

THE STOP AND GO

When we stop for the night, Cloud moves her head to the side to invite me to stand near for comfort in the dark. I turn away. If I'm not free, there is no consolation in company. I lie down in the dust and wish for the earth to swallow me.

It does not.

In my dreams I am chasing the horizon with Storm at my side. But it is Cloud who wakes me, and the human who forces me to stand. I keep going, numb to the sparkle of the hovering bird and the chirp and buzz of the yellow-headed blackbird and the red glow of morning.

But as the day wears on, a little curiosity sparks to life in me. "Where are we going?" I ask.

"To your Stop," Cloud says.

"My Stop?" I ask.

"You will live at a Stop now. They aren't so bad," Cloud says.

"When will we get there?"

"When we're finished with the Go."

I blow a loud snort against this Stop and Go nonsense.

"No one knows why humans travel from a Stop to a Go," Cloud admits. "Eating happens at the Stop. Running happens in the Go. There is no running at the Stop and no eating in the Go."

That makes no sense at all. A smart horse stops every time he finds a promising patch of food. But all day long we canter past good food, and we don't stop once.

We cross a gravelly stream. The water is slow and warm like all the rest of the streams, but a few mouthfuls is better than nothing. The hills are like the ones by my home waters. Grass and sage on the lowest parts, leafy trees in the middle, and needle trees above that. We stop at the top.

An enormous lake lies ahead, sky blue, with mountains behind it. Not round-topped mountains like home. Sharp gray mountains all white at the peak. Taller than clouds. I've never seen them so close before.

As we get nearer to the lake, humans crowd together on the path. Some ride horses. Others sit on loads pulled by draggers. The human in the brown wrapper makes that bird chirp, and just like before, Cloud goes from a walk to a steady lope. For the first time in my life, there is no joy in running. The human chirps again, and Cloud runs full out.

I keep up.

"The faster you run, the better they treat you," Cloud calls as we gallop.

When at last we come to the Stop, I'm hot and sweaty and itchy. I want nothing more than to find a dust patch and have a nice long roll. A human with gray mane meets us. He's clearly the stallion of

the place, by all his shouting. A bay human in a tan wrapper unties me from Cloud and pulls me away. I wonder if I'll ever see her again. She's not my friend, not like Fire. But still.

"Go on," Cloud says. "I'll come check on you after a while."

The human leads me around to the back of a big cube. There's another one of those wooden caves and a trap. The human waits, to let me take it all in. Tall trees sway in the wind beyond the yard. They block the view of the horizon. I give them a look-sniff. No claw beast. Still, I'd feel safer in the open.

The human walks me back and forth in front of the wooden cave. It's very dark in there, but I can smell a horse. Not Storm. Not Mother. Nor any horse of my band. I'm glad not to smell them. Happy they're still running free.

The horse in the cave is drowsing. Alone. No friend to lean on. No bandmate to watch his back. These ridden horses are a mysterious bunch.

"You there! What is this place?" I call.

Deep in the shadows, the horse opens an eye, sighs, shifts to another foot, and sleeps again.

The human walks beside me, he on his back legs and I, more sensibly, on all four. He makes a buzz like a whole hive of bees, lower and then higher and lower again. My lifebeat slows to a steady walking pace, and the human brings me to a standstill. He looks inside and then back at me. I blow hard against the idea of going in. I will do no such thing! A horse needs his sky!

I give him a loud snort to say so. I kick out and tug against the line. The human ties me to a post and leaves. The line is not very thick, but much tougher than it looks. Maybe I can bite through it. I've only begun to nibble at the knot when the human is back with water.

Water.

A horizon and water are all I need.

I drink deep. And while I do, the human puts a grabber on my neck. I shiver, but I'm too thirsty to move away. His grabbers work into the itchy spot right at the base of my mane—the spot where Storm always gave me a nibble.

How does he know?

I huff in surprise, and he huffs right back. Under the tan wrappers, he's a dark bay, and his mane is short and black. I sniff him.

Woodsmoke. Ashes. Dry grass.

He makes the beehive sounds again. He moves slowly.

This human is probably like an old stallion who has lost his band. I've seen them walking alone across the hills. Waiting at the water for everyone else to drink first. Sometimes a pair of them travel together. But most spend their days alone. There's no harm in them. I huff again, but I do not fear him.

He uses his grabbers to make nibbles along my mane. It's been days and days since someone has given me the nibbles. After that he strokes my neck and shoulders firmly in big circles. Dirt and grit and itch bugs let go of my skin and fall off.

It feels good. Wonderful, even. He does the same all down my back, and I only twitch a little when he gets close to my burn mark.

He brings me more water afterward. Now that it's twilight, I can see into the cave better. The horse sleeping inside stirs.

"So you're the new one," the horse in the shadows says.

"I'm Sky," I say.

"Call me Blaze," he says. "Safer inside than out," he adds, and then takes a big mouthful of dry grass. He's bigger than me. Hard to judge his color in the dim light, but the white blaze on his face is clear to see.

"A horse needs his sky," I say firmly.

Blaze chews for a long while, looking me up and down. "Suit yourself," he says at last. "You're a wild one, aren't you?"

I don't know what it means—wild. I only know that I'm in a strange place far from home. Every hoot and rustle of the bushes makes my heart race. Every harmless scamper and night bird grows enormous in my imagination. I face them, but then some bitty creeping thing starts chewing at the dried grass in the cave, and I turn again to make sure it's not some fearsome beast that only sounds small but is actually huge and full of teeth.

The stars open their bright eyes in the darkening sky. The moon rises and sets, but I do not sleep.

CHAPTER FOURTEEN
THE GUIDER

A blackbird sweeps down from a pine at the edge of the forest and perches on the post beside me. The morning light gives a green shimmer to its black feathers. It's the largest blackbird I've ever seen.

"Watch the blackbirds," Thunder told me when I was small. "They will see trouble where you cannot."

I keep a respectful distance and watch. The blackbird has its eye on the place where the humans went the night before. I've already guessed that trouble will come from there. Soon the bay human comes out. He's eating from his grabber. The blackbird lets out a soft rattling call, like water over stones. It bobs its head up and down.

Trouble.

The human makes a low chuffing sound of his own. He rocks his broad shoulders side to side as he walks. He bares his teeth quite fiercely.

Do humans bite?

He takes some crumbs of what he's eating and puts them on another post. The blackbird flies to it, gobbles them down, and flies off with a quick caw of thanks.

Maybe not trouble?

I look the bay human over carefully, wishing the blackbird had been more specific.

The human lets me loose inside the round trap. I eat the grasses along the edge while he brings out the sleeping horse—the bay with the white blaze on his face. He's not tied as I was. He doesn't run away. And he has a clear chance! I check, and sure enough, there's a burn mark on his shoulder just like mine. So there is no hope for him either.

Blaze looks older than me. He's tall, but his mane and tail don't have a single tangle or twig, which makes him look like a newborn foal.

The human brings a jangly loop of lines out of the cave.

"Look out!" I call. "Danger!"

Blaze gives me the sort of snort you'd give a newborn foal who startles at every little scamper and scurry.

"It's a guider," Blaze says. "You'll get yours."

The human slips the guider up over Blaze's head. Part of it goes around his nose and another part goes along his cheek and over his forehead and ears.

I don't like the look of it.

Next the human spreads a wrapper over Blaze's back and puts a perch on top. A strap for the perch goes under his belly. Blaze winces a little when it's pulled tight. Still, he doesn't punch or kick. As soon as the perch is firmly in place, the human reaches into his wrapper and pulls out a short, sharp stick. He gives it to Blaze, and Blaze eats it! In one bite!

"What was that?" I ask. Sticks are what you eat when you're starving.

"The pointy treat," Blaze says, munching happily. "Delicious! Sweeter than flowers! If you do something well, there's a treat. Sometimes a round treat, or best of all, a small crumbly treat."

The human fills a box with water and leaves Blaze standing by it.

Then the human gets into the round trap with me. I dodge away from him, trotting along the edge, but it brings me right back to him. I turn around, but I can't get away. I look for a place to jump out. A spot with open ground to land on. The trap is shoulder-high. I know I won't make it.

Storm was always making up jumping contests. I have a keen appreciation for the height of a shrub I can jump over, and I've earned plenty of cuts and bruises from the shrubs I cannot. Even so, I lunge toward the rail. My shoulders slam into it with a loud crack.

Pain shoots up my ribs. I scramble back to my feet.

"That's not the way to get a pointy treat," Blaze says.

I pay no attention to that stick eater. I'm sweaty and hungry and sore. The human stands in the trap with me. Quietly. His front legs hang by his sides; his head is tilted down. I spin away from him again and again, but he's always there.

Calm. Quiet.

I do like calm.

I pause for a moment. He waits without moving. I circle away and come back. Blow an angry breath at him.

"Let me go!" I say.

"The only way to ever run again is to let the human be your bandmate," Blaze says. "It's not so bad. There will always be food."

"A human bandmate?" I toss my head at the very idea. Who would choose these slow, skinny creatures? Not me!

Every time I circle back, he is the same: calm face, tan wrapper, short black mane. Finally I stop and give him a closer look.

He takes a long, slow breath.

So do I.

His eyes are brown, dark brown like my mother's.

No! A human cannot be a bandmate. I stamp the ground hard against the idea.

He draws a line in the dirt with his foot. And then he stands still again. He makes that bumblebee sound.

"They will bring you water," Blaze says.

I'd be the bravest horse that ever lived if only I was not thirsty.

"Nobody likes a rider, but you get used to it," Blaze says.

I look the human right in the eye. I take a step toward him.

He holds out the pointy treat.

I give it a sniff.

A lick.

Another sniff.

And then I take it right out of his grabbers. It crunches like a stick but tastes as juicy as a new spring leaf. And sweet. So sweet!

"This tastes amazing!" I say. I swallow it down and give a sniff to the human's tan wrapper in case there are more.

"Told you they were good," Blaze replies.

Maybe he's right about all of it.

After I finish my treat, the human lets me look at the guider and then puts it around my head. He moves slowly, making that bumblebee sound the whole time. Dark clouds roll in. When the wind shifts, the human stops and lets me look around and smell for danger. Then he goes back to fitting the guider snug over my forehead, under my chin, and around my nose. I shake my head hard, but the guider doesn't come off. I lick at the part in my mouth, but I can't push it out.

The human holds on to the guider. He comes right up to my face and strokes my nose. He gives my cheek a good scratch. I blow out a thoughtful breath. I don't like the idea of the guider. Not at all! But it doesn't hurt.

Before I have a moment to get used to the feel of it, there's a slight tremble in the ground.

A running horse!

I turn my ears forward and back. What danger is the horse running from? Is it just one? Many? I taste the wind for smoke. A moment later I hear the clatter of hooves coming toward me. One horse. Just one. Coming at a dead run from the sunrise side of the yard. I jerk the guider out of the human's hands. I circle the trap. How will I get away if it's the claw beast? What if it's fire?

"The rider is coming," Blaze says.

"What rider?" I ask. "Why is he galloping?" A sensible horse only gallops from mortal danger.

The human brings Blaze to the middle of the yard.

"Settle down, you wild one," Blaze says. "Humans run to something, not away from something."

A red dun gallops into the yard. He skids to a stop, sending up a cloud of dust. In the blink of an eye, the rider is off him. A stiff brown cover lies over the dun's perch. The rider lifts the cover off and slaps it down over Blaze's perch.

Blaze shuffles his feet. "Not too bad, nothing heavy," he says. He looks at the sky.

"Rain is coming," the red dun says. He shakes his head hard enough to make the guider rattle.

A human comes out of the Stop with something for the rider to drink. Steam rises from it, and it doesn't smell like water. The rider drinks it down in one gulp.

"Is this the chestnut rider with the short temper?" Blaze asks.

"The same," the dun says, breathing hard. "He's better when they feed him." He turns his back on the rider in scorn.

Both Blaze and the dun give the humans a hard stare, to remind them about the food for the rider. The humans stand there jabbering like jays and pointing to the clouds that are getting darker by the moment. Then the rider hops on Blaze.

My heart races. What does it mean, he's better when they feed him? Better than what?

I poke the bay human in the shoulder, and he takes a round thing with a hole in the middle out of his wrapper. He puts it in the rider's grabber. The rider takes a huge bite and chews loudly. He caws like a blackbird, and Blaze bolts like he's seen a slither. In a flash they're gone, and all I can hear is the sound of galloping hooves growing fainter. Rain clouds thicken and hide the sun.

"Wind run beside you always," I say a little sadly, because I was almost ready to like Blaze.

"Wind run beside you," the dun says, breathing hard. "My old stallion said that to me when he ran me off. You must be one of the wild ones."

CHAPTER FIFTEEN
THE PERCH

The red dun walks beside the human, catching his breath and cooling down. The human strokes his tawny neck.

"What do you mean, a wild one?" I say to the dun.

"I mean no harm by it," he says. "Some horses will look down on you. Them that were born inside like Blaze." He points with his lips in the direction Blaze ran off. "I only mean that you were born under the sky. Like me."

"Is it bad to be a wild one?"

"The ways of humans will always be strange to

you," he says. "The horizon will always call your name."

I close my eyes and swallow hard. I have all the water I need, but none of it tastes like home.

"My band is from that way." I point stormward. "Not far," I say. "I could find my way back."

The human lifts the perch off the dun's back.

"My home waters are far," the dun says. "Too far. And I've been gone too long to ever find them again."

He sighs as the guider comes off. Shakes out his black mane. "What do your own call you?" he says.

"Sky."

"Mine called me River."

The human rubs away the grit from River's coat. He works a tangle out of his mane. Dark clouds and the low growl of thunder come closer. I close my eyes, hoping the rain I can smell is falling on my home waters. On my band. On Storm.

"What's it like at your home waters?" I ask.

"We lived stormward," River begins. "A fine open

place. All the horizon you could want. Humans never came there."

"Is there a single mountain?" I ask, remembering Fire's stories.

River nods. "Steep on the sunrise side," he says. "With a swift river, not too deep to cross, and a salty white desert."

"Is it far?"

"Yes," River says. "Very far."

The human brings dry grass for River.

"We have a better life here between the Stop and the Go than many horses," River says, chewing as he speaks. "We're better fed than many. We always have a roof against the rain."

"How can you stand to have a rider?" I ask. "On your back, like a claw beast!"

"You get used to it," River says. He moves his head to the side, inviting me to share his food. "If you stay calm and run hard, they'll like you."

I cannot imagine it. Still, River looks well fed. And Blaze.

Cloud too.

I take a bite of the dry grass. River has the same burn mark as me, but no other fight mark on him.

"Take a rider and run fast with him," River says. "That's the whole game. Play it well, and they will trust you."

The human leads River into the cave and unties him. Just like Blaze, River doesn't try to escape.

The wind picks up. The smell of the coming rain wakes a longing for home in me as sharp as a slither's bite.

"How do you get them to untie you?" I call to River.

"Be worthy of their trust," he answers. "Be steady."

I resolve to become the most trustworthy horse that ever went from a Stop to a Go.

My plan is put to the test immediately. The human comes out of the cave with a perch in his grabbers. First, there's a wrapper.

It's flappy.

I do hate flappy things!

Still, the way to freedom is to endure. I press my lips together and endure. The human gives me firm strokes all down my neck. He brings the perch close, where I can get a good look. I nudge it.

Hard as a rock, but smooth.

Be steady, I tell myself. *Be trustworthy.*

The human swings the perch up and over my back and settles it midway between my shoulders and hips. I shudder from nose to tail. Dodge away. Look all around for danger. But it's just me and the human, alone in the round trap.

Thunder growls, and then rain begins to fall.

At last! The first rain of winter! I lift my head and say my thanks to the sky.

"Water is strength," Mother always said.

"Water is strength," I murmur as the rain rolls down my face.

Birds keep a moment of quiet to honor the rain. Even the trees breathe out their pine-scented gratitude.

The human turns his grabber up to the rain until

it holds a puddle. He touches the water to his face. Together we breathe deep. In that moment I like the human. He's older than me. Strange in so many ways, and yet he loves the rain. Just like me.

I come back to his side.

Resolute.

The human takes out a long strap. He touches me under my belly as if to say, "This is where this piece of the perch goes." I don't like to be touched on my belly. I press my lips together and look hard at the human, so he'll know to be careful of my tickle spots.

He only touches my tickle spot once, and I only step on his foot once. He gets the idea right away. Apparently a human can learn a thing. You wouldn't guess to look at them.

He pulls the strap tight and then tugs at the perch to see if it will fall off. I rear up in front and kick out in back to show him what a good job he's done making the perch snug. He steps back in admiration. Once I'm still again, I get a pointy treat.

He leads me around in circles, and then he brings a big bundle of something out of the cave. He sets the bundle on my back, and the weight of it makes my lifebeat race. I imagine the weight of the claw beast. I dodge to the side and look over my shoulder, just to be sure no danger has dropped on me. Then we walk in circles again. After a while I barely feel the weight.

When at last we're done, the human takes me out of the trap. He ties me to the post. I stomp my foot against the unfairness. Even after all that work, I'm not trustworthy enough to be untied.

CHAPTER SIXTEEN

THE RIDER

It rains all day and the next. Riders come and go. The dust settles. Hard dirt gives way to mud. We practice wearing the perch again. I hate the feel of it, but I learn not to panic at the weight.

When they aren't running, Blaze and River are full of advice.

"They'll point your head in the way they want you to go."

"When they tap your sides, they're ready to run."

"They will moo like a dragger and pull up your head when they want you to slow down or stop."

Every time I feel the approach of a running

horse, I turn my ear to the path. The human sees me do this and turns his whole body to listen. It must be hard to hear anything with such tiny ears.

Blaze gallops into the yard, all spattered with mud. The rider is a palomino with a pale mane and blue eyes. He wears a head cover and a long, soggy wrapper.

"Wet road," Blaze says, breathing hard and shaking the water from his ears and mane. "But the rider's steady. He won't give you trouble."

"Rider? Me?" I glance from Blaze to the human. "But I've never—"

The rider takes his perch cover off Blaze and slings it over my back. It's cold and damp, but not heavy. The rider drinks the steaming not-water. He shakes the rain off his head cover.

"Where will I go?" I ask Blaze. "How far is it?"

The bay human sees I'm anxious and gives my neck long, steady strokes.

"Lots of up," Blaze says. He takes a drink.

The rider gives my cheek a pat. He checks my

perch strap to see it's tight. He hops onto my back as quick as a bird. I stagger to one side and then the other to get my balance. I swallow hard against the flutter of panic from having a living creature on my back.

And then they untie me from the post! I can go. Go! At last!

The rider makes the chirp-chirp sound, but I barely hear him. I sprint out of the yard in a flash, across the meadow, toward my home waters, kicking up my heels for the joy of being free to run.

The rider shouts. He clings to the perch.

I'm determined to be steady. To run hard. Just like they want. I splash across a creek. I dodge around a tree and blink against the rain. We've barely started when the rider pulls back on my guiders in a way that makes it very hard to be calm or go fast.

"They said go fast," I remind him, keeping a steady pace in spite of the pulling.

The rider does not listen to me. He pulls my head up and back.

Very frustrating.

I shake my head against the pull. Home is in front of me. I know the way!

But the rider keeps tugging the guider.

The guider.

Is he trying to tell me something? I slow from a sprint to a gallop to think about it. The moment I slow down, the rider eases off.

Interesting.

I speed up again, and he pulls my head back. I slow to a traveling lope, and he eases off.

Fine. A steady lope then.

The rider tugs at my mouth with the guider again. I slow to a trot. But the rider keeps slowing me down until I'm only walking. I blow out hard in frustration. It will take forever to get home at this pace.

The rider gives my neck a firm pat, and then he pulls again, but this time only on one side.

It turns me right around.

I turn myself back toward home. The correct direction.

Perhaps the rider was frightened by how fast I can run. A human can barely run at all. I begin with an easy trot.

The rider bounces on the perch. Very unpleasant.

I move to a gentle canter, but there's the guider, stopping me again. Turning me again. I stop, ears back to hear what this rider has in mind.

He makes the chirp-chirp sound.

There must be some mistake.

I turn in a full circle so that I'm facing home again. I walk this time. Very sedate. No bouncing.

Still he pulls on the guider and turns me away from home. He moves me back toward the path.

The path leads straight up the mountain.

"Mountains are no place for a horse," Mother always said, when Storm dared me to go.

"Dangerous!" Auntie Gale said firmly.

"Bitter cold," Auntie Rain added.

I glance back at the rider. He gives me the chirp-chirp again. He taps my sides. Blaze did say I should go up. To be trustworthy, I'll have to follow my rider like I would a lead mare. I blow hard against this fate. I look over my shoulder toward my home waters. And then I head toward the mountains.

I get another pat from my rider. He stops pulling on the guider. I look up, up, and up at the steep sides of the mountains. They don't look so big from far away. Up close, they are taller than clouds.

The rider relaxes his legs, leans forward, and makes a hiss like a slither.

I break into a full gallop. After so many days of walking and then standing still, I love the stretch and pull on my muscles. Love the rain on my face and the wind in my mane. The rider lets out a yip, and we fly along the path to the mountains.

CHAPTER SEVENTEEN
OVER THE PASS

The path to the mountains is level at first, but it grows steadily steeper. The rider and I fall into a rhythm. He leans a little bit to one side or the other to guide me around puddles and boulders. Nobody on the path is as fast as me. Most humans are walking. Some have unhappy burros laden down with heavy, clanking bundles. No wonder Old Jack wanted to take his family far away.

As the path gets steep, the rider slides his grabbers lightly along the groove of my neck. I can feel my lifebeat against his touch. The rider leans back slightly, and we slow to a brisk trot. The white-trunked trees with the flappy yellow leaves stand in huge groves beside the path.

At first I'm impatient with the slower pace. But as we rise higher into the clouds, my breath comes short. The path switches back and forth as we rise. Inside the cloud, I can only see a few steps ahead. It's not raining anymore, but wet clings to my skin. The pines along the path are tall and narrow. When we break free of the clouds, I blink against the sudden brightness. I hold to a brisk trot as the path narrows.

A huge blackbird flies alongside me. Its tail feathers tilt from side to side to hold it steady in the rising air.

Trouble, I think.

I glance around for danger. It lets out a caw that echoes off the mountains. A sheer drop appears on one side of me. I veer away from the edge. The rider lets me walk. Sings to me like a bird as I gather my courage. I look up and see a cleft in the mountain peaks. A way to pass through. And we're almost there!

When we reach the pass, the rider pulls me to a stop and we turn to look at the tops of the clouds stretching as far as I can see. My home waters are out there somewhere. Storm is out there. I'm so high up, I can look down on the soaring hunter bird. No one in my band has ever climbed a mountain.

"I will find my way home," I promise the wind.

The wind answers in raising gusts. A chill comes over me.

What if they never let me go?

I turn toward the sunset. The ground is not

so steep now, but it's rocky. Trees are shorter and have crooked trunks. A gray bird with black wings pokes its beak deep into a pine cone. It digs out a nut, swallows it, and gives a victory squawk. Shrubs spread their branches wide instead of high. Tiny red berries hide beneath the leaves. Our path winds between shrubs and boulders so that I can't run. I'm glad of it. Something about being this far above the clouds makes me breathless.

I hear a curious whistling among the rocks. My rider hears it too, and he echoes back the whistles. A little creature pokes its head above the scattered boulders. It has round ears and no tail, and a whistle like a bird. I've never seen the like.

We travel downhill now. The trees grow taller and straighter as we go. There is a small pond, but we don't stop to drink. We pass two draggers with a great load of dead trees rolling along behind them. A pair of eagles circle above a meadow, looking for scampers to eat. The path gets wider, and I get more and more thirsty. The shadows are pointing toward the sunrise when we reach the new Stop.

It looks a lot like the valley Stop, but with many more trees around it. A big human stands in front. This one is pale, with no mane at all. I smell the dry grass around the back, so I don't wait for the rider to take me there. In back I find a yard like the last place, with a rushing stream behind it. A bright bay mare with three white feet is saddled and ready to go. She's small like me and has a kind eye.

"How was your run?" she says as the rider slides off my back. I shudder with relief to have the weight of him gone. My hooves throb from carrying him so far and so fast. He lifts the cover from my perch and settles it onto the bay's.

I don't know what to say. I've never been ridden before. Never climbed a mountain. Never ever been so far from home.

The rider takes my face in his two grabbers. He shows me his teeth. I twist my head out of his grasp in case he means to bite me. He holds out a tiny brown lump that smells like a flower. I lick it, and it melts like frost, but it's sweeter than any flower I've ever tasted. The zing of the sweetness lifts my mood and my weary muscles.

"He's a good rider," I say to the bay. "I hope I see him again."

"You will," the bay says.

The rider gives her a pat and then hops onto the perch. They gallop toward the sunset, leaving me alone in the yard with the smallest human I've ever seen.

CHAPTER EIGHTEEN

THE COLT

The young human at the mountain Stop is not so much small as lean. Big ears. Big feet. But skinny as a sapling tree, a buckskin human with a black mane. He looks like one of the piñon gatherers, though there's not a piñon tree in sight. His voice is as light as a songbird. He is too big for a yearling, but he is definitely not of fighting age. A colt, then.

The stallion of this Stop has a deep, coarse voice like a blackbird. He caws at this colt of a human, who leads me past a long wooden cave that's open along one side. Four mules are at one end of it. They grumble to each other as they eat.

"Same stuff as always," says one with a gloomy shake of the head.

"But with more grit and gravel in it," says another.

"Not a patch of clover for ages," says the youngest of them.

"Rain today. Rain tomorrow," the oldest one says.

They acknowledge me with turned ears and quick glances. Sometimes a burro family has a mule in it. They're steady fellows and strong, but seldom cheerful.

The human colt leads me to a stream, swift moving and cold. He shows me a slow eddy where I can see the bottom clearly. I wade right in. Ah! Cold water on your feet after a hard run. The best feeling! I drink my fill. The colt picks up a small stone. He tosses it over the still part of the stream. It bounces off the top of the water twice before it lands in the forest on the far side.

Good trick!

I watch him sort stones until he finds the right kind and does it again.

A game!

Humans can play!

I listen to the rush of the stream. Watch a tiny gray bird dive under the water and back out again, shaking the drops from its feathers and gulping down the water bug it has caught.

When the stallion of the Stop caws at us again, the colt runs back to the yard so fast I have to trot to keep up. He ties me to a post and then lifts off the perch. What a relief to breathe in a full breath! He takes off the guider. I'm so glad to have that thing out of my mouth, I lick him right on top of his head!

He works all the mud and sweat out of my coat with a scratcher. It's much colder up here than at the Stop below. I'm glad to have my sweat wiped away.

Afterward he gives me a handful of crunchy bits. I lick his grabbers clean.

The shadows grow longer. The colt

puts dry grass inside the cave. My mouth waters at the sight of it. Still, the dry grass is inside and I'm outside—where a horse should be. He leads me toward the cave. The back and sides of it are closed, but the front is open so it's not as dark inside.

The colt walks into the nest. He comes back out again. He takes my face in his grabbers. His eyes are dark brown like Storm's. He slides his grabber up the side of my face and over the top of my ear. He rubs the edges of my ear, firmly but tenderly—like my mother used to when I was small.

My neck and shoulders relax. I've been holding them tight for days, bracing against one new thing after another. I'd be tired even if I hadn't climbed a mountain today. There isn't a scrap of fresh grass in the yard. I blow out a big sigh. A horse has to eat. I give the sky one last look and step inside the cave.

It's dimmer inside but not too dark to see. I check, just in case a claw beast is hiding.

It is not.

The colt leads me to a nest full of food, and I

go to work on the pile of dry grass. It's gritty, as the mules said, but I'm too hungry to care. He watches me eat for a bit, and then he goes off to scoop piles out of another nest and carry them away. He wipes off my perch and guider and hangs them up. He goes to the mules with handfuls of crunchy bits.

"Thank you," the mules murmur to him softly. "Thank you kindly."

They nuzzle his shoulder and blow gently on his ears, the way you do to a true friend. They invite him to eat. He's a hungry-looking thing.

He goes inside the Stop when the mane-less human calls, but he's back soon enough. He shows me how to turn around in my nest, so that I'm facing the open end. We stand close together and watch the sun go down. The clouds glow pink and purple. I murmur my thanks to the sun for warmth and light. He rests his head on my shoulder. I've missed this so much—a friend to lean on at the end of the day.

When it's dark enough for stars, the colt walks to the very edge of the yard. He climbs up on a rail and

places his grabbers around his mouth.
He makes a hooting sound exactly like
the call the night bird makes.

Hoo . . . hoo—hoot! Hoo . . . hoo.

He waits.

Listens.

Hoots again.

Waits.

At last he comes back to the nest. He puts his front legs around my neck and breathes hard as if he's been running. He gets a salty smell, and sure enough there's salt all down his face.

I give him a lick until all that good salt is gone. I thought he would go inside, like the other humans do, but he stays with me. He makes a pile of dry grass nearby. He pulls a thick wrapper around his body, and soon he makes the long, slow breath of sleep. He is young to spend a night alone with none of his own to guard him. Perhaps he has strengths I cannot see. I breathe softly upon him and hope it's true.

CHAPTER NINETEEN

ROUGH RIDE

The next morning the air is sharp and cold. The salty-faced colt gives me a good scratch along my neck. He leads me to water. There's a rim of ice along the edge of the stream. Songbirds flit from branch to branch, gobbling up seeds and berries as if it's a race to eat the most. I'd be content to stay at the stream all day, drinking, listening to the birds, and watching the colt hop stones across the water. But a ruckus at the Stop brings us back.

Mules drag a load into the yard. This load has people inside and bundles on top. The humans get out and go into the Stop. I don't know why.

A smell of burning wafts out of the place.

The colt and I are left alone with the load and the mules. He unties the first two mules and brings them to the stream.

"Good morning," I say to the remaining mules. "How was your run?'

"Run!" the first mule snorts. "You are the only runner here."

"We plod," the other mule says. "We only plod." He shuffles his hooves in a footsore way.

"All up," the first one groans. "Up all morning!"

"Just a little more up," I say. "And then a whole lot of down."

"Down is hard too," the first mule says.

"Don't care for the down at all," says the other.

Their long ears droop. They don't have a perch on their backs, but thick straps circle their shoulders and connect to the load. I would hate to have that heavy, creaking, swaying thing always following at my heels. No wonder mules are so grumpy.

The colt settles all four mules in the cave. Then he brings out the ones who'd been grumbling all night long. He puts the strap around their shoulders. He ties them to the load. He strokes their noses.

"Be brave," they say to him. "Be steadfast."

And the colt understands, because he lifts his head and stands tall.

But when the other humans come back, he curls his shoulders in and looks at the ground. They walk right past him without a single nod or greeting. They climb into the load and leave—the mules grumbling with every step.

At midday I hear a horse at full gallop. The colt hears it too, because he sprints to my side with the guider and perch in his arms. He has them on me in a flash. He tightens the last strap as a rider, on the same bright bay mare from yesterday, gallops headlong into the yard. The rider is a gray, with pale eyes and speckles across his face. He springs off the mare. He's angry and shouting, though I can't guess why. The mare is kind and gentle. Anyone can see it. The mane-less human gives the rider some not-water, all steaming in the cold air.

"He's an angry one," the mare says. "There's no escaping the sting."

"The sting?"

I hate wasps. Everyone does.

"The faster you run, the sooner he will be off you," she says.

I shuffle my feet. The colt strokes my ears. He touches his nose to mine and breathes deeply. I do the same, and my confidence grows. I can go fast. Fast is my best thing.

The rider eats great mouthfuls of something. Nobody has fed the colt, not all morning long. What kind of a band is this? My family always feeds the foals first.

No mare. That's the problem. A mare knows the way to go and how to care for everyone along the way.

The rider gets on my back. I stagger to regain my balance and fight off the urge to panic at his weight. I blow out my fears and run. We retrace the way from the day before. The path is wetter because it rained in the night. I try to keep to the edge where it isn't so slippery. When I check my stride to keep balance, the rider stings me on my rump. I rear up in surprise, but he clings to me like a thorny twig. I resolve to make this the fastest run ever, so I will be done with this rider.

As we get near the pass, the ground becomes rockier and less slippery. I speed up, but as we round the little pond, I smell something.

Something bad.

Something ahead of me.

I slow in spite of the stings from my rider. Is it a claw beast? I swing my head from side to side. Turn my ears to listen for the smallest hint of danger. There are no trees to hide in, but there are tall boulders all along the path.

It's the claw beast, I'm sure of it! It passed this way in the night.

The rider can't smell the beast. He urges me forward. Punches my sides with his feet. Hits me

with the stinger. My lifebeat races. Maybe the claw
beast is still near.

"Trouble," I tell him, plain as day.

He ignores me. Speed is my only chance.
I leap forward, galloping to the crest in the
trail. I don't pause for a moment to look
down at the big lake. I want this rider off
my back as soon as possible. It's drier
and less slippery on the downhill side.

I take the switchbacks at top speed, dodging other travelers. I'm hot and thirsty by the time I get to the flat, but I don't let up.

I'm weary to my bones when I turn off the path and into the yard of the downhill Stop. I want to lie down and roll over on top of the speckle-faced rider, but I'm so tired I'm not sure if I could stand up again. For the first time I understand what Thunder means when he complains of creaky knees.

The bay human is there with Blaze. The rider hops down from my back, takes the perch cover off, and puts it on Blaze. In a flash they are away.

The bay human and I walk circles around the yard. He has fight marks just above his grabbers. I wonder what creature attacked him long ago.

"It was awful," I say to him because there is no one else to tell. "A claw beast in the mountains. And I was all alone."

Every day, for days on end, I've missed my family with a dull ache like the cold. But now I miss them sharp, like a broken bone.

The bay human's grabbers are as thick and rough as the colt's were thin and smooth. He runs his grabbers firmly along my aching shoulders.

"What if the claw beast is there tomorrow?" I look at the mountains, all cold and gray, and blow hard against that fate.

The bay human turns. He blows out in the direction of the mountains. He looks at me as if he knows all about fear and loneliness.

He gives me water. He takes off the perch and wipes away all the mud and sweat. He takes a close look at the spot where I brushed against a thorn bush. He pours water on the cut and spreads a sharp-smelling mud over it. He puts me in the nest. He ties me there and goes inside.

I have never been so tired. I ran all that way. I kept my rider safe from the claw beast, and still the humans don't trust me enough to untie me. How will I ever get free? I feel the tug of the homeward horizon, and no amount of water or crunchy bits will make me feel better.

CHAPTER TWENTY

FIRST SNOW

Between the Stop and the Go, one day is much like another. The colt is always there to greet me at the mountain Stop. The valley Stop always has the bay with his calm and steady ways. I miss Storm every day, but I find comfort in the company of these humans. I grow stronger and faster on the dry grass and crunchy bits and plenty of water. The riders give me treats when I run well, and a few of the riders give treats to the colt when the mane-less human is not looking.

Cloud and her rider come through whenever the moon goes thin. They bring a load of dry grass and salt and other bundles for the Stop. Her rider checks the legs and feet of every horse and mule, and Cloud frets about the drafty cave and the mountain cold as if she were a mare of my own band.

The same horses come and go each day. I begin to think of them as trusted friends, carrying news from other horses of the path.

"First snowfall coming," the bay mare warns.

"Thieves on the flat," Blaze frets.

"We lost a rider," Cloud says. "But the horse came through."

I run the same Go every day. Sometimes in daylight. Sometimes after dark. Each day is colder and windier than the last. I still haven't seen the claw beast, with its sharp teeth and its bloodthirsty thoughts, but I smell it every run, and sometimes its tracks cross my path. Howlers hunt on moonlit nights. One morning I come across the bones and antlers of someone who did not run fast enough.

The riders change from one day to the next, so I don't have to endure the angry rider every time.

Most riders wear a bright red wrapper and a cover on their head. Most of them carry a black thing that clicks on a strap around their middle. Sometimes they take it out and shout and wave it at humans who block the path. Sometimes it clicks, and then all the humans hop out of the way, lifting their front legs in the air as if it's a game.

Most riders have a firm hand and a kind eye. Some sing or whistle in the Go. Others cough and sneeze and shiver. Some wave and call out to fellow travelers. Some scowl and keep silent. All of them—every single one—is tired and hungry. I see it in the way they gulp down the steaming not-water and tuck bits of food into the pouches on their wrappers.

Sometimes their heads bob as they ride. Sometimes they get looser and looser on the perch, and one time a rider fell right off me. I swerved at the last minute so he would fall on the nice, soft mud in the middle of the path and not the hard, rocky edge. The rider did not thank me for this. He shook himself and climbed back on, grouchy as a mule for the rest of the Go.

I pay attention to the feel of a rider after that. When one of them goes all loose in the saddle, I say, "Steady now. Almost there."

It's not their fault. I can rest when we come to the Stop. The riders keep going. Nobody ever brushes their coats or tends their feet or gently rubs their ears. After a while I grow to care about the good riders and look forward to our runs together.

My coat grows thick in the colder weather. Rain rolls right off. The dry grass and crunchy bits they feed me keep my belly full and my blood warm. The riders grow winter coats too. Long and gray usually. They put covers on their grabbers and wrap a long and flappy thing around their necks and noses. Sometimes a rider tucks a stiff and cold grabber under the perch and presses it against my back until it grows warm again.

Humans are chilly creatures—no fluff or fur to them at all.

When light flurries of snow fall at the lake, heavier snow falls as we climb. Then the birds hide away. Hardly a scampering thing shows its face. But when we get above the clouds, the world is glittering bright. Birds sing, and bounders, in their winter-white fur, hop across the top of the snow in spite of the cold.

One snowy morning, the rider pulls me back to a walk. And then a complete stop.

They never ask for a stop.

Ahead a bear lumbers toward us. A bear! I seldom  saw them in my own home waters, but Auntie Gale loved to tell stories about them. A bear is fast for such a roly-poly thing, but this one is not running. It is standing like a human. The rider takes that black clicker off its strap. The wind blows toward us, so I get a full blast of the bear's sour dead-fish-and-dirt smell.

"Not to be played with," I murmur quietly, in

case the rider's mother has never told him so.

The rider points the black clicker straight at the bear. The bear sways from side to side. It huffs and grunts.

The rider pees right there on the perch, which they usually do not.

The bear gives one last grunt and drops back down to four legs. It must not like the smell of human pee. I don't care for it myself. It crosses the path and disappears into the snowy ferns and shrubs beyond.

When we get to the Stop and the salty-faced colt takes off the perch, I warn him about the bear. I speak to him plainly. It's the best I can do.

The wind picks up that night. The air grows bitter cold, and my breath turns to white smoke. The colt has a fur from a bounder wrapped around his neck. He has more fur wrapped around his legs, front and back. It gives him a nice bounderlike smell. He stacks bales of dry grass to make us snug against the wind. I lie down, and he curls up so close to me that I hear his lifebeat. I think of my family, as I always do at night. I imagine them gathering together in the lee of a hill. Standing in a circle with the foals in the middle. Moving to the waters at dawn to kick at the frozen edges and keep a drinking spot open. Together and safe as horses should be.

But not us. We are alone—the colt and I—and fearsome things stalk our dreams.

CHAPTER TWENTY-ONE
THE CLAW BEAST

Snow falls steadily through the night, and a great winter hush comes to the forest. In the morning, snow stands shoulder-deep in the yard. But I am warm and dry, even without my family standing close by for comfort and shelter. Snow covers the path completely. No rider comes. No humans walk or ride past. Tiny birds with black heads and peeping voices hop across the top of the snow. The tree scamper glides from tree to tree, nibbling at cones and disappearing into a hole in the trunk. The mane-less human comes outside. He hitches the four mules to each other.

"Don't want to!" says the lead mule.

"Not sensible!" the oldest one insists.

"Won't!" the younger ones shout.

He doesn't listen. He holds all four guiders in his grabbers and walks behind them.

"Too cold!" the youngest wails.

"Slippery!" the oldest one warns.

The human drives them into the snowbank. They push and push against the snow. Grunt and groan. Slowly they make a way, almost a tunnel. I hear them struggling and complaining with every step. But soon the great silence that comes when the snow falls thick and deep returns and wraps around me and the salty-faced colt.

While the big human is gone, the colt creeps inside and comes out with a mound of food. I'm glad to see it. He never gets as much as the others. He eats the food slowly and carefully. Not a crumb falls to the ground. He saves the red treat for last. He bites into it, and a burst of sweet smell floats my way. It's like a field of flowers in the middle of winter. Juice runs down his chin. He eats around the edge but gives the best part, with all the seeds, to me.

The sun is setting when the mules come back. They are weary and crusted with snow. The human's nose and ears are red as berries. He makes a fire in the middle of the yard. I've never seen a fire in the wintertime. I marvel at it from a distance. The mules stand close as the snow melts and steams from their sides. The big human goes inside, but he comes back out shouting. He grabs the colt by the ear and forces him inside. A moment later we hear him howl in pain. The mules and I keep our eyes on the ground and press our lips together tight.

When the colt comes outside, there's a fight mark on his face. He's shaking from head to foot. I don't understand. A stallion only fights another grown stallion. He waits until his colts are big enough to survive alone before he drives them away. The salty-faced colt is no stallion to be sparred with. He's far too tender for such rough treatment.

Still he is gentle with the mules. He melts the icicles out of their manes and brushes snow off their backs. The mules thank him tenderly, and we all wish a swarm of stinging wasps upon the bad human; may he never sleep in peace.

The next morning the bay mare comes in. I ride out with the palomino rider. It's bitter cold and still and bright. The pale-blue sky and the blinding white of the snow dazzle my eyes. The path is packed hard by the work of the mules yesterday, but it's still slippery. We go at a walk. A blackbird lands on a branch and shakes snow down on my back. I shiver at the warning and check the shadows of the forest for danger. When we get to the summit, with its

stunted trees and tall
rocks, I pick up the
scent of the claw
beast.

It's strong.

"Look out,"
I say to my rider.

I stop. Search.
Listen.

There!

I nose point.
The claw beast
is on a rock that
overhangs the path.

Watching. Hungry!

"Shhhh, shhh, shhhh," the rider says.

I shudder with dread. Look all around for an escape. Before the snow, I had space to run. Now deep drifts surround me, and the only sure footing is on the path. We should turn back. But never once in all my time with a rider has a single one turned around.

The rider takes the clicker off his belly. He holds it steady in two hands. I edge back, legs shaking. The claw beast lashes its tail. It casts its golden eye upon me and crouches, all ready to spring.

"Shh, shhh," the rider says again. He breathes out hard against his fears, and I do the same.

Craaack!!!

A burst of thunder comes from the rider's hands! Right over my head. My ears ache from the sound! I feel the echo of it in my bones.

I hear a wild scream, a dull thud, and then a dying snarl on the path ahead.

I rear up.

The rider jumps clear.

I slip on the packed snow of the path and tumble over into a drift. The human takes my guider and pulls my head above the snow. A bitter, burned smell clings to him. I thrash and roll until my legs are under me again.

The claw beast lies on the path in front of me. Completely still, as if fast asleep.

I shy away. A claw beast has many tricks.

The rider strokes my neck to settle me. I feel his grabbers shaking. He goes to the claw beast with the clicker in one grabber and a long stick in the other. He gives the claw beast a poke, but it doesn't move. He drags it by the tail to the side of the path.

He holds my head in his grabbers and looks me in the eye. He makes that *shhh, shhh, shhh* sound again. His eyes are the color of the sky. His grabbers are cold and shaking. His lips are pale. He walks beside my head, so I don't have to see the fallen claw beast or the smear of red in the snow.

But I smell death. I know the smell will live in

my memory until the end of my days. Already the blackbirds gather, their harsh voices shouting death. Howlers will come too, with their sharp teeth and their hungry families. It could have been me coloring the snow red.

But not this time. Not today.

The rider climbs back onto the perch. We go down the mountain as fast as I can. My thoughts are a whirlwind. They do not come to a rest at the valley Stop, where the bay human gives me extra rubbing. He checks my feet with care, offers a double portion of crunchy bits. But my thoughts are still in a tangle.

The palomino rider is the best, the kindest of them all. He protected me from the claw beast. And yet thunder and death came from his own grabbers.

Death in the space of one lifebeat.

Death without a fight or a chance for one side to back down and slip away.

"The best fight of all is when no one throws a kick," my stallion told me when I was still a foal. "Better to scare off a challenger than to defeat him."

And so he had stood tall and bared his teeth and showed his strength many more times than he actually kicked or bit a rival.

That was fair. I wanted to be like my stallion.

And this rider—with the pale mane and sky-colored eyes. This one who sings like a bird. This one who saw that the salty-faced colt was hungry and gave him food. This one who is the best of them all carries death in his grabbers. How can I ever trust any of them? Every rider carries the black clicker. The angry rider and the sleepy rider and the kind rider alike. They can give death to any creature in an instant, with no fight at all.

I do not understand. I only know that no matter how kind a human might be, I have to get away from them all. I have to find my own band. My own way. My own home waters.

CHAPTER TWENTY-TWO

WAITING FOR SPRING

I think about my escape all night long and for many days to come. I eat their treats, the pointy one and the round one and the crumbly one that's the sweetest of all. I'm grateful when they scrub away the mud. I get used to the shelter of the cave. They stop tying me to a post in the nest at night. But when they close the rails, they slide a thick stick across to hold the gate shut. I watch carefully as the salty-faced colt in the mountains and the bay human by the lake shut the nest tight. Slide-*thunk* to close. *Thunk*-slide to open. Always the same.

One night when I have a full moon for light and

the colt is off at the edge of the forest hooting like a night bird, as he does every night, I try moving the stick myself. It takes some work with my tongue and teeth to get a grip on the thing, but once I do, it slides easily. I push the gate open with my nose. Stretch my neck for a look and take a step out.

Freedom! A proud shiver runs up my neck.

I go to the mouth of the cave. The snow is beaten down on the path, but off the path, the snow is high and smooth and sparkling in the moonlight. Little scampers leave star-shaped tracks over the ice-crusted top. I'm too heavy to run on top of the snow and not heavy enough to break a path alone. My only chance to escape lies along the path, where surely the riders who travel day and night will find me.

The riders could kill me as easily as they killed the claw beast. If the snow was gone, I could hide.

I'll have to wait for the snow to melt.

The days wear on. Snow falls upon snow. Stories of horse thieves and fallen trees and rumblings from deep underground travel from one horse to the

next. Blizzards howl in from stormward. Travelers
are few and nights long.

In time the days lengthen, and the trees shake

off their icicles. The steady *drip-drip* of melting gives me hope. Snow still covers the ground, but underneath it, I hear running water.

One evening, just as the colt finishes brushing me, I get a whiff of something strange. It comes from the forest and not the path where new smells usually come from. It isn't the smell of a horse, nor any rider I've met. I turn an ear to the shadowy spaces between the trees.

"Trouble," I murmur to the colt.

I point, but I don't think he can smell anything. A human has such a tiny nose. Only useful for sneezing. He looks where I'm pointing. But if he sees something that I can't, he doesn't say. Nothing stirs in the forest, so I go into the cave at sundown. I eat. Drink. My winter fur is letting go, and I rub against the rail to work off the itchiest bits. The colt goes out as always to make his call to the night bird.

Only this time, the night bird calls back.

CHAPTER TWENTY-THREE
THE CHOICE

I peer out of the cave into the dim yard. The colt hoots again, and the night bird calls back. Again. The colt glances at the light shining out from the Stop. He bares his teeth quite fiercely. Peers back into the forest. Then he turns away from the trees and hippity-hops on his way to the cave, like stallions do when they're sizing up a challenger.

Odd.

Not like him at all.

He feeds and brushes the mules, same as always. Strokes their fuzzy ears and kisses their noses. He goes in for food and comes back out. He brushes me carefully and scratches my neck just where I like it.

The moment the light in the Stop goes out, he puts on every wrapper he has, even though it's the warmest night yet. He doesn't curl up in the nest. He doesn't breathe the slow breath of sleep. He waits, eyes wide open and teeth bared. He hops from one foot to the other, ready for a fight.

The smell comes back . . . the one I noticed earlier. A human appears out of the darkness. He's tall, with a black mane. The colt throws himself at the stranger, locking his front legs around his neck. He's immediately swept off the ground. I've never seen the like. My colt, who shrinks away from every human, is attacking the biggest human of them all!

The bigger one holds him fast. They don't snarl or bite. They hold each other tight and say nothing. I cannot tell who is winning.

At last the larger human sets him down. They speak in whispers. And then the pair of them walk out of the cave and into the shadows of the forest. They don't take the path. The big one sweeps the soft snow behind them so that their tracks don't show. They go silently. They do not look back.

The mules lift their heads and murmur to each other.

"Gone," the lead mule says.

"Sad," says the other.

"They've come for their own at last," says the youngest of them.

"Wind run beside them," says the oldest, with a heavy sigh.

"Will they catch him and bring him back?" I ask.

We all turn an ear, hoping that no one inside wakes up.

"If they choose me to chase after him, I will lead them the opposite way," the oldest mule says.

"Opposite is the best way," the mules say as one creature.

I look into the forest, where my colt has disappeared.

"Don't be hasty," the mares of my band have told me a thousand times.

"Look first and then run."

"Smell first and then decide."

I ignore all that good advice. I do not think for one moment how it will be after I'm free. I only know that the salty-faced colt is free of this Stop, and I can be free of it too.

I grab the latch in my teeth. My lifebeat runs at a gallop.

Thunk!

Slide!

The gate swings open. A shiver of joy goes up my legs.

"Danger!" the oldest mule warns me.

"We could all be free," I say. "We could never carry a rider or pull a load again."

I can still smell the colt and his kin. They're traveling deep into the trees. I move silently to the mules' nests and open each one. The youngest of them steps outside, but then freezes, full of doubt.

"The human inside this Stop is the worst of them all," I say.

"Cruel," the mules agree.

"Grit and sticks in the food," one of them adds.

"Fought the colt," the oldest says sternly. "Fought to the red, and him full-grown."

"We could give that bad human someone else to chase," I say. "If we all go in opposite ways, we can give our colt a chance."

The mules put their heads together. They discuss.

"Opposite is the best way," the oldest announces.

And with that, all four mules go out. They make rings of tracks around the Stop. Their hooves sink deep in the soft spring snow. Two go down the path toward the sunset and two take the sunrise way, leaving clear tracks to follow. They kick up their heels and break into a trot.

"Out!" says the lead mule.

"Done!" says the other.

"Never again!" they shout.

Soon there is nothing left of them but the fading sound of their feet.

"Wind run beside them," I whisper to the night.

I turn my back on cold and loneliness and the weight of the rider. I gather my courage. I call to memory the waymarks that will lead me home.

I've barely begun my journey when I hear the horse and rider coming up the path in the dark. I sniff the wind. It's River. I freeze. Look for cover. A shout comes from the rider, and a shuffle of hooves on the slushy path ahead.

"Where are you going?" River asks.

"Away!" shouts the oldest mule.

"Far!" says the youngest.

A moment later, I hear the heavy tread of mules at full gallop.

"Opposite is the best way!" the mules call out as they run. I breathe out softly in gratitude for the steadfast kindness of mules.

River and the rider keep going, as the riders always do. They head toward me at a steady lope. I look for an opening in the trees and plunge into the deeper dark of the forest.

"How could they have gotten free?" River says

to his rider as they come. "Brave choice for a mule."

The rider says nothing. They come closer and closer. I hold as still as a stone. The moonlight casts deep shadows in the trees. When River catches scent of me, he slows ever so slightly.

"Brave Sky," he says softly as he passes my hiding place. "If only my own home waters weren't so far."

He travels on without turning his head to betray my hiding place.

You know the way! I want to call out to him. *You are strong and fast. You could find your home waters if you try.*

I remember all that River and Fire have told me about their home waters. *Run stormward, beyond the big lake, across the dry steppe for days upon days. A single mountain with a white sand desert beside it.* I want to shout those memories to River, but fear keeps me silent. Fear, and a new-kindled hope of freedom.

The sounds of River and his rider fade away. If I keep going, I'll never see him again. He's not just a friend, but one who was born wild like me. I want him to come with me. What will happen to him when I'm gone? Already freedom is not easy.

I will never forget him, I promise the stars.

I'm ready to run, but which way? The forest hides me, but it's thick with ferns and shrubs and plants I can't even name. I cannot run in the forest. I can barely walk. And I don't know the way. On the path I can run. On the path I know the way. On the path they will hunt me.

"Keep away from the trees," the mares of my band would warn me when I was a foal. They told me dreadful stories about the claw beast and all the fearsome creatures that lurk in the dark. But I have faced dangers they never imagined, and the fearsome creatures of my life walk about in broad daylight.

When I imagined my escape in the long nights of winter, I dreamed of galloping over open ground, not creeping through the forest like the smallest scamper. A chill wind runs down my back. I'm not so fluffy as I was before.

If I choose the path, I'll get out of the mountains faster. It will be warmer down by the lake. But I will be hunted on the path. I remember the sound and bitter smell of the black clicker that the rider used to kill the claw beast. Death in an instant. Death that even I cannot outrun.

If Storm were here, she'd choose the way for me. She wouldn't hesitate. But there is only me. Sky. Not the tallest. Not the strongest. Certainly not the wisest. I don't want to choose. I'm afraid to pick the wrong thing. I feel rooted in place in the trap of my own caution.

I close my eyes. The bumblebee song of the bay human fills my memory. I can feel the gentle touch of the salty-faced colt. Their kindness in my memory steadies my lifebeat.

"Speed is my strength," I whisper to the trees.

I remember all I have learned about the Stop and Go. The path is usually empty at night. When River and his rider get to the mountain Stop, and no fresh horse is ready, they will go on to the next Stop. The bad human will have to chase me and all the mules on his own legs. Human legs are not for running. Even a roly-poly bear can run faster. I have at least until the sun rises before anyone with a horse to ride knows I'm gone.

I shake off fear. I choose the path.

CHAPTER TWENTY-FOUR

A STRANGER

I step out of the forest. The moon casts its light, but trees still make deep shadows across the path. I listen for danger. I call on the wind for speed, and I run. I pass the still-frozen pond, the bones of the claw beast, and the stunted trees and icy boulders of the summit. I catch the pungent smell of a bear taking its first peek out of its den. I take the downhill switchbacks at a steady gallop. If it were day, I could see the large lake and all the waymarks I have held in my memory all this time.

Without a rider, I can run forever.

I know the way. I will find my home.

I chant it as I run. I promise it to the stars.

It's still dark when I reach the flat. I leave the path before I get to the valley Stop so that they won't hear me and send a rider out after me. I cross open meadows clear of snow and dotted with pine. I pick out my waymarks in the moonlight. My confidence soars as I pass each one. I pause only once to drink at a stream. I take a quick roll on the soft ground, but no amount of rubbing will wear away the burn mark on my shoulder. The moon is setting, and dawn will bring humans and danger.

I cannot be taken. I will not endure it again.

I pass the end of the big lake and turn stormward.

Familiar ground is ahead! My family is ahead!

As the sun rises, humans with heavily laden burros and draggers with their rumbling loads start to travel on the path. I keep off it. I hide in the trees when I see or smell humans coming. I go at a steady lope when the way is clear, stopping only to eat and drink. My thoughts turn to Storm. I know if I keep going, I'll come to hill shapes I'll recognize.

The soft ground holds news about who's gone by. I see tiny star prints of songbirds and the long, narrow footmarks of bounders. After a while I find a new track. It has two parts like a pronghorn. I take a sniff.

I've never smelled anything like it before.

The track is far too big for the pronghorn. And the space between each step is very long.

A shiver runs up my legs. Anything with such a long stride is either running very fast or is very tall. I search each mark carefully. They are level. A running track would be deeper at the front. Tall, then. Very tall. No horse alive has a stride as long as this.

Still, all the creatures I know with two-part tracks are grazers like me.

"The more parts to a track, the more danger," Mother always said.

The bird with the curved beak who hunts slithers has a four-part track. Howlers and claw beasts have five. I have open horizon all around me. I'm not worried. I can outrun anything on open ground. I follow the tracks. The wind blows steadily in my face. I don't like the dust in my eyes, but I love being able to smell the new creature ahead. The smell grows stronger. The mysterious creature will be over the next rise. I approach with caution. When I get there, I do not see the new creature at first because it is holding still and because it is the yellow-brown color of bare dirt. Then it takes a few steps. Something is very wrong with the shape of it!

Four legs, good. But so long!

Bulgy knees. Big feet.

Its round body looks strong, but it's the wrong shape. Instead of a straight back—level from hip to shoulder—this fellow has a great bump! Like a tiny mountain that it carries everywhere it goes. I'm mesmerized. It grazes on sage. Takes a few steps. Grazes some more. It does not have claws. It hasn't howled yet. I walk a little closer.

"Hello, new creature," I say when I'm still a long way off. It's not nice to sneak up.

The creature looks at me, blinks, and goes back to browsing.

I can't help myself. I have to take a closer look.

The creature's neck is long and curved like a water bird. It's all one color—no spots or stripes to give it interest. I walk right up to the creature.

"Hello," I say again.

The creature opens its nose, breathes in the smell of me, and then closes up its nostrils again as if they are eyes.

Good trick!

It has long lips and small round ears like a bear

and a double row of black lashes on each eye. It holds my gaze for a moment. Then the creature turns away and lets out a deep, throaty growl. It spits a glob of sticky water onto the dirt in front of me. A bitter stench rises from the glistening blob.

I do not know this game.

Sometimes a scamper will leave a seed or a nut for another scamper to eat.

I will not eat the blob. It is making my eyes water.

The new creature makes another growl, even longer and louder than the last. I make a nervous nicker of my own. None of the aunties have a warning or even a story about this creature. But the stink does give me an idea. I lift up my tail and drop the smelliest pile I can.

The new creature does the same and then turns and walks away.

It's not a very good game.

I don't care for it at all.

Still, I am sad to see the creature go. Like me, it is all alone in the world. I watch until it disappears in the distance.

I press on, footsore and lonely, and by the end of the day the hills look both more familiar and more strange. The shape seems right. Everything else is wrong! It's quiet. No birds in the air or scampers on the ground. Not a pronghorn in sight. I break into a gallop, but my unease grows more intense with every step. I don't see or hear or even smell another horse. I know the shape of this land like I know my own name. But the trees are gone.

Every last one.

Knee-high stumps as far as I can see.

I've seen a forest after a fire—blackened trees, scorched ground. Grasses and shrubs gone. But new growth always sprang up after the winter rain and snow. The tall purple flowers and the pines grow first, and the mares say all the rest comes back in time. Here only the trees are taken.

Sage is left. Grasses and flowers, tall as ever.

I remember the day, only two seasons ago, when Storm and I saw a human cut down a piñon. It filled me with dread then, and it was only one tree in a forest that stretched as far as I could see. Now there's nothing but stumps and a bitter smell in the wind.

My lifebeat races. Who did this? And why? There's not a creature alive who does not love a tree—for its shade, its food, its sound in the wind, its beauty in every season.

At the end of a long life, a horse gives his body to the earth and his breath to the sky. It's a sorrowful time for a band. We stand beside our own until the last closing of the eyes. We breathe in his last breath. It is hard to bid farewell to the fallen. Even so, it feels right to stand watch.

I listen among the bones of the forest, and I wonder if a tree takes a final breath. I stand watch over the largest stump—a grandmother of piñons. There's nothing to say, but my anger grows. And my fear for my family. I stomp the ground. Lash my tail from side to side. There's no fault in lightning. No malice in a flash flood. But this was done on purpose, just as I was stolen from my home waters on purpose.

I touch my nose to the grandmother stump. I breathe in deeply to gather my courage. I close my eyes. I don't know what to wish for a creature who cannot run.

"Rain fall upon you always," I say at last.

I walk until I come to the remnant of my home waters. I drink with gratitude. It is warm and quiet with no trees for shade and cover. All that day I linger by the water, waiting for my family to come out of the hills and drink.

No one comes. Not my family. Not a single horse or burro.

At the Stop and Go, I dreamed of going home, imagined my family safe along this shore. I never thought my home waters could change so completely.

It must have rained recently, because the orange rain-flower speckles the hillside like stars. Bees and flutters of every color go from flower to flower. The quiet unnerves me. I keep looking for what I can't hear.

Into that silence come far-off sounds. Clangs and booms. Whooshes and rumbles. Most of the noise comes from the top of the ridge. I go to see what could be making such sounds. As I draw closer I don't just hear the rumbles and booms, I feel them in my feet.

Sometimes the ground moves. All creatures know it. Some say a monster lives down there—the mother of all claw beasts or something even more sinister.

My mother always said, "The ground has its thunder, as does the sky."

These rumbles sound different. Feel different. When I gain the high ground, I cannot believe my eyes.

CHAPTER TWENTY-FIVE

THE DIGGERS' CAMP

A foul-smelling fog rises up from a hillside below me. It is crawling with humans who are digging holes. The skeletons of trees lie strewn about. Entire streams have been dug up and moved.

One path runs through the middle of the diggers' camp. Blocks along the path have humans going in and out like at a Stop. Some of the blocks are just frames covered in flappy things so much bigger than the flappy bits a human wears.

Horses and riders come and go on the path. Draggers pull their loads. Just beyond the blocks are traps filled with horses and mules and burros.

Dark holes spot the ground. Mounds of rocky earth are piled beside them. Diggers trudge in and out of the holes. Humans of all sorts shout and wave their front legs at each other. Round pits filled with broken rocks are beside the dark holes. Each pit is stirred by a horse or burro dragging a rock crusher in circles. Next to the pits, fires smoke and sputter. The horses and mules who grind the stones stumble with weariness. They cough in the foul air. Peril and destruction is all around. Not a speck of shade or shelter remains. The horses who aren't working wait in the round traps with heads low.

I turn away in horror. I breathe in and blow out over and over, but the nightmare of what I've seen won't leave me. The smell of the place already clings to my mane. I want to run. I want to put as much space between myself and this ruined husk of a hillside as I can.

But all those horses. Trapped. Just as I was. Suffering so much more than I ever did. What if my family is there?

I pace the hilltop. The rattles and bangs of the

diggers' camp float up on the wind. The jumble of human voices are loud, but sometimes I hear the horses.

"I cannot take one more step!"

"So thirsty."

And even more softly . . .

"Come lean on me."

"Hush now, night is coming."

"Soon they will sleep."

And then I hear shouting. Many diggers shouting all at once, and the high and shrill scream of a mare in pain.

I know her! It's Storm! I search the crowd of humans below.

"Get! Off!" Storm screams. "Now!"

A grunt, and a thud follows, like the sound a falling human makes. And then more shouting.

I do not plan.

I do not wait.

I do not think two steps ahead of my own feet. My family is what I have saved my strength for.

I gallop down the hill at top speed. I turn onto the wide flat path. Humans stand on wooden walkways on both sides. Horses and burros and draggers and loads crowd the path.

At the far end is a round trap. Storm's gray head and white mane rise over the heads of the diggers. One digger balances on the rail of the trap, ready to jump on her back. Another lies on the ground just outside the trap. Moaning. Most of the humans are drinking sour-smelling water. All of them are shouting. Except one.

One human is calm. One human is quiet. He has a thick black mane that's messier than most, but wrappers that are cleaner than most. He stands off to the side with a twig in his hand. He scratches across a stack of flat white leaves. All around him humans are sparring, but he only has eyes for Storm.

There are several horses on the path. Some have riders. A team of six big mules is hitched to a load.

Several small humans sit in the load. Larger humans add bundles and tie them down. How can they all stand by when Storm is hurting?

"Help her!" I shout as I run.

"Too late," says one mule.

"Cannot be helped," says another.

The horses look the other way, ashamed.

"We're stronger than humans!" I shout. "If we fought them together, we could win!"

"Never been done," says the lead mule.

"Risky," says her partner.

"Humans are quite flimsy," insists the rear mule. "We could hurt them if we tried."

I dash past them. I crash into the human trying to mount Storm. He flips right over the rail and onto the dirt. Storm steps on his chest, and a great whoosh of air blows out of him. She stumbles when she steps on the line that winds around her neck and drags on the ground. The crowd moves back. A few stagger and fall down. I bite and kick at the ones who remain. Storm does the same, and soon not a single human is hanging on the rails. The man with the wild black mane sets down his leaves and pulls the fallen humans out of the way.

"Sky!" Storm gasps. "You came back!" She takes a step toward me, wincing in pain. Cuts run red all down her shoulders. I touch my nose to her cheek.

"Look at that," the rear mule says. "'Tis a matched pair they are."

"Matched indeed," agrees her partner. "Pity the one is free and the other is not."

I circle the outside of the trap, looking for the secret latch, ready to impress Storm with my ability to open it. Before I can find it, a human comes toward me with a line twirling over his head. More humans swarm out of the blocks. My burn mark is in plain view. They could capture me. They could send me back.

"Now you've done it!" shouts the lead mule.

"Made it all worse!" agrees her partner.

I will not go back. Never!

I charge the human twirling the line. He staggers back, but others are right behind him.

"'Tis wrong how they treat the filly," says the middle mule.

"'Tis ashamed they should be," agrees her partner.

They put their heads together and confer in low tones.

"Fear not, young filly!" the mules call. "We come!"

The lead mule yanks the line free that holds the team to a post. They walk toward the trap, pulling their load behind them. The little humans tucked in among the objects shriek like sky hunters. They bounce and beat their grabbers together.

"We come," the mules say again as their load rolls down the path, gathering speed.

"Fear not, wee human foals!" says the rear mule, giving the youngsters a glance.

"'Tis wrong to harm the young," her partner says. "Never shall we harm you."

Horses all along the path stand aghast at this show of independence.

"Lot of spirit for a team of mules," a grulla horse says to his fellows.

"Who would have thought?" says a blue roan.

"Trouble will come of it," a heavily burdened burro insists.

"Trouble is good," says a younger burro. "Trouble is what we need."

The mules gather speed. They steadfastly ignore the shouts of humans. They fix their eyes on the trap, and I guess their plan.

"Stand away from the rail!" I yell.

Most of the humans have guessed the plan too; they are staggering and sprinting away. The human with the wild black mane walks up to the rails. He reaches for Storm's neck. I bite his front leg. At the last moment he jerks away, so I only get a mouthful of wrapper. I spit it out, but he's back at Storm's neck quick as lightning. He takes the line in his grabbers, loosens it, and slips it off her head.

I give a sharp snort of surprise.

He looks me in the eye and snorts right back, as if to say, *What a band of scoundrels these humans are!* And then he blinks one eye at me and disappears into the crowd.

"Down it shall come," bray the mules. They break into a trot. They meet the rail with a loud *thunk*. They push until the rail bends and then snaps. The tiny humans shriek, even higher and more shrilly. The rails do not stop the mules any more than a spider's web would. With a final groan and crack, one side of the trap lies flat on the ground.

"It is done," says the lead mule with a satisfied huff.

"Thank you," Storm says. She leaps past them and onto the path.

"Fare thee well, truehearted friends," says the rear mule.

I touch my nose to hers in gratitude.

"Fare thee well," I say.

And then I race after Storm.

Humans are not well suited to running. They do not run willingly up a hill. Storm picks a particularly steep and rocky slope. I glance behind. One or two ambitious humans run after me, lines a-twirl over their heads. Most just watch us run. Laughing, many of them. In the midst of it all, the mules stand tall, tails swinging, heads bobbing with satisfaction at work well done.

"Fare thee well, sisters," I say again, and I scramble up the slope after Storm, leaving the smoke and the stench and the cruelty far behind.

CHAPTER TWENTY-SIX

WATER BEFORE EVERYTHING

Storm stands in a cluster of sage and piñon stumps at the top of the hill, breathing deep and blowing hard. Her legs shake with fatigue. The fight marks where she was struck are still fresh and oozing. Worst of all, she's lean and bony. She never looked small to me. Never. She was always the strong one. The brave one.

I approach her slowly, but she turns away as if I'm a stranger.

I don't know what to say. My time at the Stop and Go was hard and lonely. But my home waters were a shining star in my memory. A comfort in the dark.

Some humans were unkind to me, but most were gentle. Except for the sly one with the wild black mane, I didn't see a gentle human among the whole vast herd of diggers. I blow hard against the lot of them. They are thieves. Not just horse thieves, but tree thieves, water thieves. We stand in the bones of our home waters, and all the life in it has run dry.

"Water first," I say softly. "Water before everything."

Storm looks away from me.

"The water has gone bad," she says. "It smells strange. Tastes different. It steals away your strength and makes you stagger."

I give her a neck nibble, but she flinches. Pain wraps around her like a trap of its own.

"Snow, then," I say.

I try to remember the shaded crevices where snowbanks lingered long past winter, but the land looks so different now.

"This way," Storm says.

She leads me toward the nearest seam in the hillside. Sure enough, at the bottom lies a glistening white cache of snow. We hurry down and plunge our heads into the icy slush. Except for the pine needles, it's delicious. We lick and crunch and slurp our fill.

Storm heaves a great sigh.

Before she can say anything, I blurt out, "I'm sorry! I should have come home sooner. All this time I thought you were free."

Storm snorts loudly. The broken stumps of what really happened are all around us.

"I would have escaped sooner if I'd known," I say.

Storm snorts again, but not so hard. We make silence, letting the sun warm our weary shoulders. All my life Storm has sheltered me and led me. I want to take care of her, but she's proud. I've never successfully made her do anything she didn't already want to do.

"I should have taken them all away from our home waters the very first day, when the human killed a tree," Storm says. "After I escaped the trap, I ran straight home to save them. I tried. But all they would say was 'Where will we go?' And I didn't know where to lead them."

I stay close, but I don't touch her. Storm is far beyond anger, and maybe there's nothing I can do to comfort her. She tells the whole story about how the humans took everything—killed the deer, hunted the pronghorn, cut the trees, stole the water and even the stones from the streams.

I rock as I listen. Side to side. I remember how the colt at the mountain Stop tucked his head down and made a turtle shell of his body after the bald human had been cruel. Only later— sometimes much later—he would uncurl and lean on my shoulder. He needed his family, and there was only me.

I try to be steady and calm for Storm, as I had been for him. But I am full of anger and thoughts of revenge. I want to crush every digger and trample them under my feet like I would a slither. I breathe my anger out like fire. I root my feet in the earth like a tree. Storm doesn't need my anger. She needs me.

I don't ask how she was captured, and she doesn't say. I listen as the shadows grow long and then longer. And finally, as the sun touches the mountaintops, I ask her what became of our mothers.

"Down by the rock crushers," Storm says. "Our stallion too."

"Then they are alive?" I lift my head. Breathe my gratitude to the sky.

"Barely," Storm says cautiously. "The crushers . . . they are brutal work. I fought it. I kicked. I bit. I refused to pull."

"Good for you!" I say, happily imagining her fight.

"No," she says. "Bad for me."

She turns so that I get a full view of her fight marks. Some are fresh, but many have been there for a long time.

"They tried to make me pull a burden. And then carry a load. In the end they made me their game." She stomps her foot hard against the hillside. "I hate diggers! I will hate them forever."

"There is a place," I say. "A safe place. My friends told me about it. A single mountain standing alone with a river of clear water to drink."

Storm swishes her tail thoughtfully.

"Let's go away from here," I say. "Far away."

Her ears perk up.

"The mountain lies stormward," I say. "Will you try?"

"Can they all come?" she asks.

I think of River still stuck at the Stop and Go. And Fire. I am angry at myself for leaving them. "I'm not leaving anyone behind," I say. "Never again."

This time I think before I run. This time I listen to everything Storm can tell me about how the diggers live. I remember all I have learned about humans from my time in the Stop and Go. We make a plan together, Storm and I. It's a dangerous plan.

That evening we go to the hilltop one last time. We look at the sun setting over the ruins of our home waters. We linger side by side, knowing that we will never come back. We do not speak but breathe in every sound and smell until the last orange and red and yellow clouds fade away. There has never been such a sky.

CHAPTER TWENTY-SEVEN

TRAPS

The moon rises big and orange, casting light enough for us to find our way. I act brave, but inside I'm full of doubt. What if they catch me? What if they capture Storm? It would be my fault. I blow out hard against that fate.

We approach the camp slowly and silently.

There's less rumble and boom underground now that the sun is down. Diggers crawl up out of the holes, thick as ants. They grumble like mules as they go. Light and noise and bad smells leak out of the places where the diggers live. Many stumble as if they too have been poisoned. Some fight with each other like young stallions do. Most are lean and dirty. A few are covered in fight marks.

We wait until they are gone from the holes and grinding stones. They don't pass the night in the quiet company of their families. They don't stand close together or nuzzle a friend or keep watch over each other.

Everything about the digging is wrong. Bad for horses and mules and burros. Bad for trees, and worst of all, bad for water. I'm not surprised it's bad for humans too. But they aren't tied to posts or kept in traps. I don't understand why they stay.

"This way," Storm says.

I follow her toward the traps and grinding pits at the edge of the camp. It's eerily quiet. No call from the night bird. Not a peep from the toads. We pass a trap full of burros. No one has scrubbed away the dirt and grit of the day. Their water box is dry.

"Here," Storm says quietly, stopping by a trap full of horses of all colors.

"Mother?" I whisper. "Auntie Gale? Auntie Rain?"

Three heads lift up.

"Is it him?"

"Our Sky?"

The other horses jostle to the side so that they can come to the rail.

"I'd know you anywhere," Mother says.

She reaches over the rail and brushes her cheek against mine. She's changed. Her gleaming chestnut coat is dull. Her ear, notched. Her steps, faltering. I don't know what to say. Auntie Rain walks with a limp. Proud Auntie Gale's head hangs low.

My whole life I've relied on the strength and wisdom of these mares. They are as tall as the clouds in my memory. Now they look as fragile as sapling trees.

"You must run from here," Mother says. "Quick!"

"We will leave this place tonight," I say. "All of us, and never endure a trap again."

"Leave?" Mother says.

"Now?" Auntie Rain asks.

"Right now!" I say. "All you have to do is follow."

My teeth grip the latch. I slide it to the side and lift up. The gate swings open, but my family and all the other horses in their trap scramble away from the opening, trembling as if freedom is a fearful thing.

"Oh, my bright Sky," Mother says. "If only I could."

"Why?" I say, fighting to keep my voice low.

I look over my shoulder. The humans are not far away. Their lamps make pools of light. If one of them sees us, if only one of them raises the alarm, there will be no winning against so many.

"We must leave now," I say.

The horses behind my family shuffle their feet and murmur dire warnings.

"I will only slow you down," Auntie Rain says.

"It's enough for me to know that you and Storm are free," Mother says.

"We can all leave, and we will," Storm says firmly.

There's a long and dreadful pause, and the horses in the open trap stand as if frozen.

"Danger," they murmur to each other.

"Take Frost," Auntie Rain says at last. She nudges her toward the opening. "Frost can survive. If we stay, maybe they won't chase you. Maybe they won't miss just the one, a yearling too young to carry or pull."

Frost steps away from her mother. She's taller than last fall, but leaner too.

"I will follow you," she whispers. "I'll go anywhere."

"I will not leave without all of you!" I say. I stamp my foot at them. "You cannot stay. Look at you!"

"Hush now, Sky," Auntie Gale says. "Of course we want to go. To be free again. To know the simple peace of choosing our own way. But Rain cannot run, and your mother . . ." She blows hard in anger. "Your mother cannot see."

I stagger back as though struck. The weary set of Mother's shoulders and Rain's halting steps show me the hard truth.

Storm draws me aside. "They are worn out," she whispers. "They only need to begin, and their courage will come back to them. Go find our stallion. They are used to his leadership."

I make my way around heaps of broken rocks and smoldering pits. I come to another larger trap holding burros and a few mules. I see the black-and-white cloud marks of our stallion. He's outside the trap, tied to a post. His mane is a dirty tangle and his coat dull and dusty.

"Thunder?" I say.

"Sky," he answers with an unhappy snort. "I heard talk of a wild horse in the diggings today. Stole the fine gray mare, they said." He swings his head to the side, tugging on the line that holds him. Not hard. Not as if he expects it to break—only out of a long habit of trying without hope of success.

"Come to fight, have you?" he says. "You were not a fighter before."

A sharp bray comes from inside the trap. "Not a fighter?" Old Jack says. "Sky's family was not in danger before."

"Old Jack?" I say, peering into the gloom.

"Look how Sky has grown," Old Jack says firmly. "A stallion knows when it is time to try his strength."

In truth, I am no taller than I was before. And I am horrified to see even wily Old Jack trapped with the rest. But I feel different. Not braver or stronger. But more determined.

"I should have run sooner," Old Jack says, shaking his gray head. "And you! You should have run farther."

"Storm and I know how to get away," I say to Thunder. "But the mares are afraid to follow us. You're the stallion they trust. They need you."

I take hold of the knot holding him fast and test the curves of it with my tongue. The line is thick. I'll never break through it, but I've seen humans pull at the curve of a knot to make it loose.

"Will you help them escape?" I ask.

"Diggers will chase us," Thunder says. "They'll bring us back. There is nowhere to hide now that the trees are gone."

"We have the horizon," I say. "All we need is the will to run."

I sink my teeth into the knot and tug. It does not budge. I turn my head to tug at one angle and then another. I dig in my feet and try harder.

The burros and mules gather at the edges of their traps to watch me.

"Can he untie a line?" asks a burro.

"Good trick!" says another.

"Never work!" complains a mule. "You'll all be caught."

"With fight marks for your trouble," says another mule.

"Try," says Old Jack.

"Try. Try. Try," the burros chant.

I let go of the first loop and tug at the next one. It gives way, just a little.

"Listen," I say to the burros. "I have a plan."

The burros and even the mules turn their tall ears toward me.

"Hopeless!" says the biggest mule after I explain.

"Try!" say the burros. "We will try."

"Humans get tired at the end of the day," Old Jack says. "Many have the staggers."

"I saw it in the diggings earlier today," I say.

"There is mischief to be made with the lights they carry about," Old Jack adds.

I give the line one final tug. The knot is loose enough now to slide it up off the post.

"Go," I say to Thunder. "Lead our family away from here. Storm will show you the way."

"Will you fight them all?" Thunder says.

"Yes," I say. "But not alone."

I take a deep breath and blow against my fears. "If I do not get free, follow Storm."

Thunder hurries up the hill toward his mares as fast as his stiff old legs will take him.

CHAPTER TWENTY-EIGHT

THE FIGHT

I dash to the first of the traps. Walk around it to find the latch and work it free.

"Look at that!" say the burros. "Good trick!"

They surge out of the trap.

"Scatter," I say to them. "The diggers cannot chase us all."

I go to the next trap and the next, working them open and freeing the horses and mules and burros inside. The first group of burros slips away into the shadows and heads toward the sunrise. A pair of black horses and a gray scramble up the hillside and turn saltward. A few cower inside the trap, afraid to take a step in any direction. The tallest mule and his companions head straight for the places where humans are sleeping.

"Never!" brays the mule loud enough to shake stones. "Never again will you . . . Never!"

He takes the wrapper around their sleeping place in his teeth and tugs it off the frame. His companion turns and kicks the frame to pieces. Sleeping diggers leap to their feet and run shrieking down the path. The mules follow them, heads low, nipping at their rumps.

Old Jack takes up the cry. "Never!" he shouts. "Never again!"

He gallops up the path with his family at his side. When he comes to a lamp, he kicks it. The thing sails through the air and shatters. Sparks fly. A flame sputters to life on the wooden walkway at the edge of the main path. Old Jack runs to the next lamp and kicks again. A few of his jennies do the same before fleeing. Showers of sparks rain down. Little fires catch and grow.

In all the commotion, I search from one end

of the camp to the other for traps to open. As the crackle of fire grows, trapped horses call out to me.

"Here!" they scream. "Help us!"

I'm determined to free them all. Each latch is different. Each one its own puzzle. One trap full of mules doesn't wait for me to come. They see what's happening and push and grunt and lean until the sides of their trap fall flat on the ground. A few humans try to chase me, but I have companions now. I kick a human in the chest when he lays a grabber on me. The burros mob the next human who tries to come after me with a line.

"Never!" they shout as they circle him. "Never again!"

The whoosh and roar of the fires soon drowns out everything else. Humans spill out of their sleeping places, shouting and stumbling. A few chase after the burros and mules on foot. Some of the diggers run to put out the flames, and some just run.

I go to the trap where my mother had been. I find the tracks. Many burros and horses are determined to come with me.

"Follow the gray mare!" I tell them.

I spot Storm at the front of a huge band of horses. She is leading them through the maze of digger holes and fallen trees. Her gray coat gleams in the moonlight. They are almost to the crest of the hills. Mother and the aunties crowd close around her, and all the rest fall in behind.

I check the traps one last time, calling for the stragglers to follow. Thick smoke and the crackle of fire are at our heels as we go. We dodge broken tools and open pits. We jump over toppled trunks and dry gullies and streams. I keep looking over my shoulder for a following rider with his twirling line, but no horses are left to chase us. Some of us are hiding a limp and some of us are calling the names of lost bandmates as we go. All the clamor and stench of the diggers falls behind.

"Almost there," I say, as I nudge on the slowest ones with my nose. "Just a little farther."

"Try, try," the smallest of the burros chants, as she scrambles to keep up.

I would carry her if I could. I keep her close and nudge her along the smoothest way I can find. And when we finally reach the top of the hills, Storm and all the rest are waiting for us in the shadows. We pause just for a moment while horses and burros and mules look for their own in the crowd.

"We mustn't linger," Old Jack says.

"They may try to catch us in the morning light," I agree.

"Then we must be far from here come sunrise," Thunder says.

They both take up places beside me, and we guard the rear together as stallions do.

The burros happily chant my name as we turn stormward.

"Bright Sky!"

"Bold Sky!"

"Brave Sky!"

We were free. All of us.

The sun rises pink and promising, and the horizon calls my name.

CHAPTER TWENTY-NINE

HOME WATERS

I wish I could say that we ran all the way to the Alone Mountain, galloping boldly across the steppe, all our troubles behind us.

In truth we walked—we stumbled. For a long time after. And now here we are, still walking as the season changes from early spring to summer. We are still looking for the Alone Mountain and the promise of a place to live in peace and freedom. We are still hiding from humans who would steal those of us with burn marks away from our families. Water is scarce on the steppe, and the heat of summer is upon us.

I stand on a knoll above the band, with Old Jack

at my side. The stars are fading, and the grass at our feet is sparse and dry.

"Why does the band still follow me?" I ask him. "I'm not the biggest stallion. Many others are better fighters. And everyone can see that the mares are wiser than me."

Old Jack chews a dry sprig of sage. He does not shout as much as he used to, though his knees are more creaky than ever. "You and Storm were free," he says. "And still you came back. You risked everything and opened all the traps. We will not soon forget."

In the rising light of morning, Storm looks over the band. Assessing their strength for the day's journey. Fresh air and clean water have made all of them stronger. But some things are slow to heal. Not a night passes when one of us doesn't cry out in our sleep. The shadows of cruelty walk alive in our dreams. And the fight marks of our past will live on our skins forever.

Thunder was the first of us to fall. When we came to the edge of our home waters on our first day of freedom . . . when he could see with his own eyes that there were no humans hunting us . . . when he believed that I would fight for our band always—his lifebeat gave out. We stood watch beside him. We took in his last breath, under an open sky. No horse can ask for more.

Storm comes to join Old Jack and me on the rise. Her fight marks have faded, but her will to fight is stronger than ever.

"We are not giving up," she says firmly.

Old Jack studies the ground ahead. He is a great traveler. He can judge a sky. What a colt should learn from his stallion, I have learned from him on this journey.

"The ground is slowly rising, just as Fire said it would," he says.

"The Alone Mountain is steep on one side and gentle on the other," I say. Together we say all the waymarks we know. We check the rising sun and turn our faces stormward.

"Listen," Storm says. "Water. Fast-moving water."

I turn my ears to where she is listening. I can

hear, ever so faintly, a low rumble of water over stones. Old Jack lifts his gray-whiskered nose. He takes in what the wind has to tell us.

"That's fresh grass ahead," he says with a satisfied huff. "Green and growing."

My hopes rise. We lead the band stormward, listening for the river as we go. Mother walks with her shoulder touching my side, so that I can guide her around the holes and stones she cannot see. Auntie Rain hobbles along at the rear of the group with Old Jack, who fights to hide his limp with every step. Little Frost has grown taller. She darts away from Auntie Gale's side to pester every mare in the band.

"What's this?" she shouts, flushing a cluster of red-shouldered blackbirds into the air.

"I can catch it!" she says as she races after a bounder with black-tipped ears.

I can see by the rounding of bellies that there will be more foals for her to play with in the spring.

We keep going because I do not know what else to do.

We have come too far to give up.

The sun is high when we find a river, fast and cold but not too deep to cross. We crowd along the bank. We drink our fill of sweet, cold water.

Could this be the place? I see a little spark of hope run through the band. We travel on, faster than before. We climb steadily, and by last light we are at the peak. The sunrise side of the mountain falls away like a cliff and a round white desert lies at the base. We can smell the salt on the rising air. There is no other mountain top in sight.

"We found it!" I shout. "Our new home!"

"A single mountain, standing alone," Old Jack says. "This is the right place!"

We turn in every direction. No diggers or draggers. No riders. No troublesome sounds or rising smoke. We are alone in the wild, at last.

"I knew you would find it," Storm says.

She stands beside me. We breathe in the new smells. We check the trees for the claw beast. Already my band is spreading out, eating the grasses and flowers—some old familiar ones and some deliciously new. Old Jack is guarding his jennies as always. There will be burro foals in the spring too. And for many springs to come. Mother and the aunties and Frost graze nearby—together and safe, as a family should be.

A night bird in the tree beside me opens its yellow eye and blinks. It hoots into the growing darkness, and I remember the salty-faced colt and all the things, good and bad, kind and frightening, that have led me here.

I turn my head to the setting sun.

Grateful.

This is the place the horizon has called me to. Home. Not just a home for me, not just for my family, but for all the free horses and burros who followed us here.

Here, where the wind runs beside us. Always.

Two horses roam free.

WILD HORSES IN NORTH AMERICA

In the age of dinosaurs, North America was home to many small, jungle-dwelling, horselike creatures. As the climate changed, around 65 million years ago, the first true horses evolved. They lived in the Age of Mammals alongside the dire wolf, the saber-toothed cat, the mammoth, and the mastodon. As tropical jungles and inland seas became temperate dry grasslands, the creatures that adapted to eating grass survived. One of the surviving species, *Equus*, emerged 4 million years ago and is the direct ancestor of the modern horse.

Equus eventually migrated to Asia, Europe, and Africa. Many scientists believe that horses died out completely in North America around the time of the Ice Age, not returning until the Spanish conquistadors brought them back 500 years ago. Others believe that with the Ice Age, both humans and horses moved to the southern parts of North America and then migrated back as the ice sheets receded.

No fossil record of *Equus* surviving the Ice Age in North

America has been found so far, yet many Indigenous people of North America hold in their history the memory of horses long predating contact with settlers. Whatever happened to those ancient horses, we know that the Spanish brought many horses to the American Southwest, where they thrived on the wide-open plains.

Now, western North America contains both mustangs, who have lived wild for many generations, and domestic horses, who have escaped or been abandoned. It does not take long for a once-tame horse to find a home among wild horses and live in a band as they do. There are places where wild horses live free with minimal human contact: at Steens Mountain in Oregon—Sky's eventual home—and the Pryor Mountains of Montana and Wyoming.

In other places, urban growth and drought bring wild horses and humans into regular conflict. Sky's home waters, the Virginia Range east of Reno, Nevada, is one such place. Reno was built on top of wetlands. Much of that water is now gone or behind fences, so wild horses must travel much farther to find a place to drink.

The United States considers all free-roaming horses to be feral animals—non-native strays. They are not given the same protection as wildlife. They are regularly rounded up to make more room on the range for beef cattle. Horses die in these roundups. Others are sold to people who train them for pleasure riding or ranch work. Some are sold for slaughter, and some remain in corrals for the rest of their lives.

A herd of galloping mustangs.

The western states have endured catastrophic droughts in the past two decades, which makes the plight of wild horses much more serious. Fewer people hunt, so there are more deer, pronghorn, and elk on the range, along with more cattle. All need water. Extreme wildfires have put stress on the range like never before.

Water conservation will help everyone—humans as much as animals. Reclassifying mustangs as truly wild animals will make them eligible for protections they don't have now. Private sanctuaries can also be created, with land and water set aside just for wild horses. One such sanctuary is forming now on the land of Sky's birth. The Virginia Range Mustangs Haven will be a 685-acre protected site for wild horses that have been rescued from slaughter, so that they can live out their lives in safety and compassion. Learn more about the project at www.vrmustangs.org.

Young stallions spar for practice.

HORSE FAMILIES

Horses live in family bands, which consist of an adult stallion and one or more mares and their foals. One of the mares takes a leadership role and decides where they go and when. The stallion travels at the back of the band, where he can protect it from chasing predators. Young males, or colts, are driven out of their home band by the stallion when they are old enough to find a mate. Groups of colts form their own bands. They practice fighting until they are strong enough to defeat a stallion and take over his band or clever enough to entice a mare to leave her band and join him.

Two foals comfort each other.

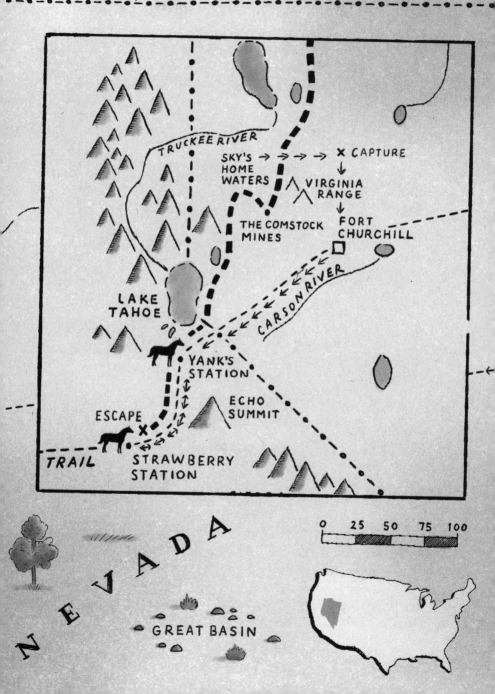

ABOUT MUSTANGS

Wild horses, often called mustangs in America, have many adaptations to help them survive in the wild.

SIZE • Mustangs stand about 14 hands tall. A "hand" is a unit of measure used especially for horses; it's equal to 4 inches. Set your hand on a ruler and you will see why. The mustangs' short stature makes them nimble on uneven ground and able to survive on less food and water than a larger horse.

COAT • Mustangs come in every color combination. They grow a thick, warm coat in the winter, which repels the rain and snow.

HOOVES • Mustangs are well-known for their sturdy hooves. They walk constantly, and the rough ground keeps their hooves healthy. Mustangs in the Pony Express did not need shoes, because they weren't carrying heavy loads.

EARS • A horse's large and mobile ears allow it to hear danger coming from all directions. Horses also use ear position to communicate with their bandmates.

EYES • Horses have the largest eyes of any land animal. Nearly full-circle vision lets a horse see a predator coming from any direction. Because their eyes are on the sides of their heads, horses can use them independently, seeing objects on both sides at the same time. This is called monocular vision. Their color vision is not as acute as a human's, but their night vision is far better.

NOSE • A mustang's large nasal cavity holds more than a thousand smell receptors—three times more than humans have. Mustangs can remember thousands of distinct smells. This helps them recognize their friends, avoid predators, find food, and retrace their steps to get home. Their large noses also warm up cold air, which keeps them warmer in winter.

SPEED • Mustangs can run 30 miles per hour. In a sprint, a mustang can go as fast as a car on a freeway.

GREAT BASIN SAGEBRUSH STEPPE

The Great Basin is the largest and most northern of America's desert and steppe regions. It's semi-arid and dominated by sagebrush, shrubs, and grasses. It occupies most of Nevada and parts of neighboring states. It is 209,163 square miles. That's a little bit smaller than Kenya and a little bit larger than Spain.

The Great Basin has snowy winters and hot, dry summers. The six-to-twelve inches of precipitation that fall each year flow not toward the ocean but inward, collecting in large inland lakes. The Great Basin is home to the Washoe, Goshute, Ute, Paiute, and Shoshone peoples, who have lived there for at least ten thousand years and live there still.

Historically, hundreds of varieties of grasses grew in the basin, making it an excellent habitat for horses, deer, elk, burros, pronghorn, and bighorn sheep. A lengthy drought in the American West has killed native plants and put stress on local wildlife, The introduction of invasive and highly flammable grasses has increased the frequency and intensity of wildfires.

The **Great Basin spadefoot toad** lives near seasonal pools and slow-flowing springs, where it lays eggs. In the spring, it makes a call that sounds like a duck. These toads have vertical pupils like a house cat, an adaptation that helps them hunt crickets and beetles at night. They have specially adapted feet for digging in gravelly soil, which allows them to escape the arid aboveground climate of the Great Basin. The toads hibernate twice a year, brumating in winter and estivating in summer.

The **chuckwalla** is a greenish-gray member of the iguana family. Chuckwallas live in rocky crevices; they resist predators by inflating their bodies to keep from being pulled out of the rocks. A chuckwalla never drinks but gets water from the plants it eats. Like the Great Basin spadefoot toad, it hibernates twice each year.

The **western rattlesnake** is well known for its warning rattle and venomous bite. The **gopher snake** is completely harmless, but it evades predators because it looks so much like a rattlesnake. That kind of camouflage is called mimicry.

Burros came to North America with Spanish explorers in the 1500s. They are about half the size of a horse but still able to carry 150 pounds of gear. This is about half their body weight. Horses can only carry 20 percent of their body weight. Like horses, burros are intelligent and form strong bonds in their family group. They can endure extremes of weather with very little food or water, and they are sure-footed on rough terrain. Though burros can run almost as fast as horses, they are more likely to stand and fight than stampede as horses do. This tenacity and their piercing voices make burros excellent guard animals for domestic livestock.

A **piñon jay** has blue-gray feathers with dark wingtips. They gather in noisy flocks of as many as a hundred. Piñon pine trees rely on jays to gather seeds in the fall. The jays eat some seeds and bury the rest, leaving a few every year to grow.

The **single-leaf piñon pine** thrives in the Great Basin's cold winters and hot, arid summers. It produces a small cone with nuts that Indigenous people of the area have harvested for at least ten thousand years. The nuts are delicious, have as much protein as beef, and they make a highly nutritious oil. They are a first food for all the tribes of the Great Basin, vital to the Indigenous communities' health, nutrition, economy, and culture.

Between 1859 and 1861, silver miners needed wood to build frames that would keep their mine shafts from collapsing. They clear-cut thousands of acres of piñon forest, which led to widespread starvation among the local Indigenous people.

Big sagebrush, commonly called **sage**, is the most abundant plant in the Great Basin. Its gray-green leaves remain on the shrub year-round, making it an important cover and forage shrub for birds, rodents, rabbits, deer, pronghorn, sheep, and horses. **Sagebrush** has a distinctive sharp, sweet smell and a peppery taste. Because it remains above the snow, sage is a staple that sees many animals through the winter. It is a vital plant for the tribes of the Great Basin, who use it for medicine, rope, and baskets.

The **dromedary** is not native to North America. In the 1850s, the United States Army purchased dromedaries from North Africa and Turkey. They were used for surveying roads across the Southwestern deserts.

THE SIERRA NEVADA MOUNTAINS

The **Sierra Nevada Mountains** are a range of volcanic mountains running 400 miles along the California–Nevada border. The Sierra Nevada range has a Mediterranean climate, with cold, wet winters and hot, dry summers. Its ecosystem changes dramatically with elevation. The lower westward slopes of the Sierra Nevada contain grassy meadows and oak trees. These foothills are called the **chaparral zone**.

As you rise above 3,000 feet and enter the **lower montane zone**, greater rainfall produces a lush forest of mixed conifers and deciduous trees, with many understory plants.

Above 7,000 feet in the **upper montane zone**, summers are short and snow remains on the ground from November to June. The forest becomes almost entirely fir and pine trees.

Only the heartiest trees can survive in the **subalpine zone** above 9,000 feet. Whitebark pine, lodgepole pine, and mountain hemlock are among the few that can withstand the thin soil, heavy snowfall, and high winds.

No trees grow in the **alpine zone** above 9,500 feet. Most of the land is covered with boulder fields and bare granite, yet even there, a few hearty plants, lichens, and grasses survive. Mammals of the alpine zone include the **bighorn sheep**, the **yellow-bellied marmot**, and the **American pika**.

The eastern slope of the Sierras is much steeper and far more dry than the western slope. Forests here feature more drought-tolerant trees, including **Jeffrey pines**, **Sierra junipers**, and **piñon pines**.

Brown bears, also called **grizzly bears**, were common in California in the 1800s. Though they are the largest predators in North America, most of their diet consists of grasses, roots, fruit, berries, nuts, and insects. They also eat fish, rodents, squirrels, deer, elk, mountain sheep, and moose. Bears eat huge quantities of food in the summer and fall, collecting a thick layer of fat to survive on as they hibernate in winter. A brown bear's sense of vision, hearing, and smell are all excellent, and because bears eat so many different things, they have impressive memories for the location and timing of each harvest, whether the food is pine nuts or spawning salmon or ripening huckleberries.

Bears have two to four cubs at a time, and the cubs stay with their mothers for as long as four years, learning all she knows about food and where to find it. The last brown bear in California was seen in 1924, but the grizzly's smaller cousin, the black bear, still survives in the Sierras. Most of North America's remaining brown bears live in Canada and Alaska.

Cougars, or **mountain lions**, are stealth predators. Though they get as big as 9 feet long and weigh as much 200 pounds, they move in complete silence. They may wait in a tree or overhanging rock for hours to ambush their prey. They kill quickly with a bite to the back of the neck, which severs the spine. Cougars eat only meat—mostly deer and elk but occasionally coyotes, mountain sheep, and raccoons. They are the only predator of wild horses.

Great horned owls are found in every American state except Hawaii, and only the **snowy owls** and **great gray owls** of Canada and Alaska are larger. They can adapt to nearly every habitat from urban to arctic, and they have the widest range of prey. Their diet includes scorpions, rodents, rabbits, skunks, porcupines, bats, house cats, ducks, geese, and hawks. Great horned owls are active both at night and during the day. Every time I have seen this owl it was because crows were swarming around it, making a racket. With its sharp beak and powerful talons, the great horned owl is one of the few predators that crows and ravens fear.

The **American dipper** looks like a plain gray robin with long legs and a short tail. It lives near fast-moving streams and waterfalls and is the only North American songbird that swims. The dipper eats insects, larvae, and fish eggs from the rocky bottoms of streams. Because they nest on streamside cliffs and even sometimes underneath waterfalls, dippers have two-part nests, with a lid to keep the eggs and babies warm and dry.

The **American pika** looks like a mouse but is more closely related to rabbits and hares. It has round ears and no tail. It lives among the rocky slopes and boulders of the alpine zone. It does not dig a burrow but rather finds a cozy crevice in the rocks to escape the hawks that hunt it. In the short

alpine summer, pikas gather grass, moss, and wildflowers, and build tiny haystacks in a sheltered spot. The grasses soon dry, and the pika fills its den with food for the long winters. Pikas often collect more food than they need, and their leftover haystacks provide nutrients to the thin alpine soil. Pikas blend in well with their rocky habitat. I have heard their cheery whistles on mountain hikes but never seen them.

Like most subalpine and alpine plants, the **mountain hemlock** grows slowly. It can be a very tall tree at lower and wetter elevations, but at the top of a mountain a hemlock can look more like a shrub, because the weight of snow and the relentless wind cause it to hug the ground. Hemlocks provide good cover for alpine animals. Their cones are quite small and disperse seeds with the wind. One way to tell a hemlock from other evergreens of the forest is to look for the tallest upward-pointing spike. If it droops over, it is a member of the hemlock family.

The **trembling aspen**, with its pale trunk and golden fall leaves, is one of the most beautiful trees of North

America. An entire grove of aspen may grow from a single root system, so a stand of aspens are all clones. They count as a single living being. The root system can endure and send up new trees for thousands of years and cover as many as 100 acres, making aspens both the largest and the oldest plants in the world.

Aspens return quickly after a wildfire. They provide food and cover for many animals, from rabbits and mice to bears and migratory birds, and their understory contains many wildflowers.

There are hundreds of types of alpine **wildflowers** on the highest elevations of the Sierras. They grow in mats and mounds close to the ground, in places sheltered from the intense winds. Most are just a few inches tall. Many have waxy or hairy leaves to protect against moisture loss and to withstand the intense alpine sunlight. Thick, fleshy roots store energy below the ground, allowing the plants to flower and produce seeds quickly in the six to eight weeks that the ground is free of snow. Because the tallest peaks of the Sierra Nevada range remained above the glaciers of the last-Ice Age, alpine flowers are among the most ancient plant species in North America.

WATER BEFORE EVERYTHING

Every living thing needs water, from the smallest microbes to the largest animals and plants. Horses need five to ten gallons a day. But a wild horse, who knows how to find small sources of water like morning dew, can survive for as many as three to six days without a full drink.

In 1860, before the city of Reno, Nevada, was built, the land at the base of the Virginia Range was a wetland—a network of ponds and streams that were filled by runoff from the mountains.

Freshwater springs were found throughout the region, fed by water from an aquifer—a body of fresh water underground. An aquifer forms over thousands of years when rain and melting snow seeps through the soil and through porous layers, such as sand, gravel, sandstone, or limestone. When the water reaches a layer that is not porous, such as clay, the water stops flowing downward and forms groundwater, or an aquifer. Typically groundwater is very clean, because dirt and most bacteria are filtered out as water passes through the soil and rock layers.

The region is also known for hot springs. A hot spring forms when magma—lava that is under the ground—heats the groundwater. The hot water and steam rise up through cracks in the rock layers and reach the surface as hot springs and geysers. Some hot springs are hot enough to kill every living thing that enters them. Others are more like an extra-warm bath. Hot springs sometimes dissolve minerals from the rocks around them, which can give the water a powerful smell. Some of these minerals are harmful to living things, but others can be healthy for people or animals who drink or bathe in the water.

When silver mining came to the Virginia Range in 1859, it devastated the environment and particularly the water—both surface streams and aquifers. When miners cut down trees to support their mines and did not replant them, the soil on the bare hills became less stable. And then as miners dug into the mountains, they sometimes damaged aquifers, causing hundreds of thousands of gallons of fresh water to tumble into the mines, destroying mining equipment and killing miners. These accidents drained aquifers. Many springs in the area went dry. The loss of groundwater damaged trees, shrubs, and grasses, which made food and shelter less available to wildlife.

The Indigenous Americans who lived in the region also lost natural resources they depended on. Many of them moved north to areas with fewer settlers and mines.

Silver and gold mining began in Nevada 160 years ago and continues to this day. It is still a disruptive and polluting process. But even in places that have not been actively mined for more than 100 years, poisons—especially mercury—persist in the water. And the places where the aquifers were drained by mining have not recovered.

Many cattle and sheep ranches have been established, and more than a million people have moved into Nevada since it became a state in 1864. Cattle and sheep and humans also need plenty of clean water. To make matters worse, climate change has brought higher temperatures and less rain, creating a megadrought that has persisted for more than 22 years. It is the worst period of drought in the American West in 1,200 years. Wild horses and burros must now travel farther than ever before to find clean water, and sometimes that brings them too close to populated areas and highways.

THE PONY EXPRESS

The Pony Express was a mail service that used a relay system of horse-mounted riders. It established stations every 10 to 20 miles, where the rider switched to a fresh horse. Each rider traveled eight to twelve stations before giving the mail to a new rider. This system allowed horses to travel at a gallop the whole way. The Pony Express route went from St. Joseph, Missouri, to Sacramento, California, a distance of about 1,900 miles.

The Pony Express began in 1860, when there was great need for a mail service between the eastern cities of the United States and its newest state, California. The US was on the verge of a civil war. President Lincoln wanted gold-rich California to remain with the US and oppose slavery. He needed a communication network that would not be controlled by the southern states who wanted to keep slaves and leave the US.

A southern overland stagecoach route took twenty-one to forty-two days one way, depending on the weather. Maritime routes that carried mail around the tip of South America usually took even longer. The Pony

Express managed to reduce that time to nine or ten days.

The mail was carried in a mochila, a leather saddlebag with four locking pouches that was placed over the saddle. Riders put the mochila on a fresh horse at each station. The transfer took less than a minute, which kept the mail speeding along.

The riders of the Pony Express were young men willing to spend twelve to twenty hours in the saddle at a full gallop, night or day, in all kinds of weather. It was exhausting and lonely work, but it paid more than twice a skilled workman's wage.

The Pony Express bought the finest and fastest horses available. Most were around fourteen hands tall, shorter than the average farm horse. Small racehorses were chosen for the easier terrain in the east and mustangs for the mountainous western sections. Mustangs were more sure-footed on the rougher trails of the West. They were better able to run at high altitudes and to withstand the cold. The horses of the Pony Express were well cared for. Still, the life was difficult, and many were retired after only a few months, so the service was always looking for new horses. The Pony Express ran from April 1860 to October 1861, when the arrival of the telegraph made the service unnecessary.

The Pony Express has become part of the myth of the West. The popular traveling circus known as Buffalo Bill's Wild West Show, which performed throughout the US and Europe from 1885 to 1913, opened with an act featuring a Pony Express rider being chased by American Indians. But though Buffalo Bill and cowboy movies suggested that Indians regularly chased the mail, there's no evidence that any rider was ever harmed or that mail was ever stolen in that way.

In the summer of 1860, during the Pyramid Lake War, a section of the mail service did shut down to replace missing horses and rebuild stations that had been raided and burned. It is impossible now to prove who conducted those raids. Many historians believe it was Paiutes who damaged the stations and released the horses. The mustangs of the Pony Express were taken from the range where Indians kept their horses. Perhaps some mustangs belonged to local tribes, who then tried to recover their own stolen horses.

If you drive across the West today, you can find remnants of Pony Express stations still standing. At Echo Summit in the Sierra Nevadas, you can hike the same trail Pony Express riders took more than 160 years ago.

SILVER MINING IN NEVADA

The discovery of gold in California in 1848 brought settlers to the American West from all over the world.

The earliest prospectors on the Virginia Range in the Nevada Territory found moderate amounts of gold. They found about $840 worth of gold in every ton of ore—less than many mines in California. But in 1859, more experienced miners thought to assess the Virginia Range ore for silver, and the value came in at $3,000 of silver in a ton of ore—more than almost every California mine produced in gold. A silver rush to Virginia City, Nevada, began.

One of the men who came to the silver rush was Samuel Clemens, who wrote for the local newspaper, the *Territorial Enterprise*. While there, he began writing funny stories about frontier life under the pen name Mark Twain. He became one of American's most famous writers and is the author of *The Adventures of Tom Sawyer* and *Adventures of Huckleberry Finn*. I could not resist giving Sam Clemens a small but vital role in my story. He is the wild-haired man who helps Storm escape.

Mining destroyed the Virginia Range ecosystem completely. Whole forests of piñon pines were cut down to provide fuel and framework to support underground mines. Water was diverted from streams to provide power to steam engines and to process ore. The water was poisoned with salt and mercury, devastating all who relied on the wetlands. Many of those lakes and waterways are still contaminated today, more than a hundred years after mining operations closed.

The Paiute, Washoe, and Shoshone people have lived on the Virginia Range for at least ten thousand years. They lived in balance with their environment. The destruction of their lands devastated their culture and economy. It was one of the factors leading up to the Paiute War of 1860 and was one of the reasons that many but not all of them left for safer territories to the north.

Mining also ruined the health of miners and the animals that worked alongside them. Malnutrition, disease, and injuries were common in mining camps.

One particularly dangerous mining machine was the arrastra. It was a simple grinding mill. A shallow circular pit was paved with flat stones and filled with ore containing gold and silver mixed with other minerals.

There was a post in the middle and a long arm that was pulled by a horse or burro. The arm dragged a grinding stone across the ore, breaking it into a powder. Mercury, copper sulfate, and water were added to the crushed rock, making it possible to rinse away all the lighter rocks. The mercury and silver combination was then cooked. Mercury vapor was collected to reuse, and only silver remained.

Mercury is a potent nerve toxin, and many miners and their animals suffered and died from mercury poisoning. Symptoms of mercury poisoning include irritability, numbness, tremors, muscle weakness, nausea, mental confusion, stumbling, and vision or hearing loss.

The population boom and the income from mining made it possible for the Nevada Territory to become a state on October 31, 1864, just in time to help elect President Abraham Lincoln to a second term, and to be an important vote in the passage of the Thirteenth Amendment, which abolished slavery in the United States.

When California joined the United States on September 9, 1850, the new state legislature passed a law often called the California Indian Act of 1850. It had many provisions that were catastrophic for the tribes of California and the surrounding territories.

The worst of these were the vagrancy and apprenticeship provisions. All adult Indians were called vagrants when they were found outdoors and not in the employment of a white person. Most Indians of the time made their living by hunting, gathering, and farming, so nearly all of them could be accused of vagrancy and taken to jail. Any white settler could pay bail for a prisoner, but in return the prisoner owed the settler up to four months of labor. Upon release from indenture, the Indian could be found vagrant again.

This is slavery. The law separated tribal members from their lands and families and made it impossible for them to keep their native languages and cultural practices.

Apprenticeship under the California Indian Act made it legal for a white settler to take any Indian children from their parents and make them work without wages until they were twenty-five years old for boys or twenty-one for girls. This is also slavery. Most children taken into apprenticeship slavery were between the ages of seven and twelve, though some were as young as three years old. There was no provision in the law to ensure that apprenticed children were well cared for. An Indian person was not allowed to testify in court. If an apprentice was mistreated, there was no legal authority to hear the complaint.

With the abolition of American slavery in 1865, some of the provisions of the California Indian Act ended. The law was not completely repealed until 1937.

The young stable hand at the Pony Express station represents one of these enslaved children. I wanted to put a human face on this historic atrocity. I have imagined for this Paiute boy a much happier ending than most apprentice slaves knew. Indian parents risked and often lost their lives rescuing their children from slavery. But Indigenous people in the American West did survive. They continue to live in our communities today. Their commitment to protecting the environment and rebuilding their culture is a testament to their strength, courage, intelligence, and fortitude.

Author's Note

I chose the Virginia Range for this story because it is a beautiful place. I chose it because it's near where the Comstock Lode—a rich vein of silver—was discovered, and because the Pony Express trail ran through it. And I chose it because it was home to a remarkable woman named Velma Johnson. She was born long after the silver mines closed. She lived at a time when more cowboys were seen on movie screens than in the wild places of the American West, a time when some cattlemen felt that horses ate too much of the forage and took too much of the water. They rounded up wild horses and sold them for chicken feed or pet food. Some people shot them for sport.

When Velma Johnson saw how cruelly wild horses were treated, she decided to do something about it. Because she had suffered from polio as a child, she had keen empathy for suffering in animals. She began writing to her local newspapers to spread the word about how badly wild horses were being treated. She took photographs and testified before courts and encouraged officials to pass laws to protect wild horses.

Powerful and wealthy men opposed her at every turn. But public opinion about the environment was changing. She gathered allies, including thousands of schoolchildren across the United States, who wrote to encourage Congress to pass the Wild Free-Roaming Horses and Burros Act of 1971. It joined a legacy of environmental laws that includes the Clean Air Act in 1970, the Clean Water Act in 1972, and the Endangered Species Act in 1973.

Together these laws saved the lives of thousands of humans suffering from poor air and water quality. They restored degraded environments and saved animals and plants on the brink of extinction, including our wild horses and burros.

I hope my readers will pay attention to the world around us and love all the wild places of the earth and the creatures, plants, and humans who live there. I hope you will love them enough to protect them. The work of reversing climate change and restoring public land will not be easy, but you don't have to be big or strong or wealthy to change the world. You don't even have to be old enough to vote. But you do have to be brave and persistent. The wild creatures of this world need your voice.

Artist's Note

From my first sketches to the final artwork, drawing Sky's journey has been a celebration of an animal I have always loved. Horses are said to be some of the hardest things to draw, but do not let this discourage you! If you'd like to draw horses, I encourage you to practice.

While working on this book, I visited many horses (and a few ponies). I recorded everything I observed, from the way they moved to how the sun reflected in their eyes. If you can meet one or two of these gentle giants in person, you too will be inspired by their majestic presence, and it is sure to shine through in your artwork.